Systema Paradoxa

Accounts of Cryptozoological Import

Volume 06
Cryptid Fight Club
A Tale of Batsquatch

As Accounted by Patrick Thomas

NeoParadoxa
Pennsville, NJ
2021

PUBLISHED BY
NeoParadoxa
A division of eSpec Books
PO Box 242
Pennsville, NJ 08070
www.especbooks.com

ISBN: 978-1-949691-67-2
ISBN (ebook): 978-1-949691-66-5

Interior Design: Danielle McPhail
www.sidhenadaire.com

Cover Art: Jason Whitley
Cover Design: Mike and Danielle McPhail, McP Digital Graphics
Interior Illustration: Jason Whitley

Copyediting: Greg Schauer and John L. French

Acknowledgments

Many thanks to Dr. Amber Dessaigne-Karwacki for her insights and knowledge of veterinary medicine that helped with several aspects of cryptid biology in this book. Any errors or extrapolations are entirely my own.

DEDICATION

FOR ERIN AND COLIN

CHAPTER ONE

"Hand over your wallet, watch, and cell phone, shrimp."

Despite the mugger's professional manner and no-nonsense tone, I had difficulty taking him seriously. This bozo better not make me lose the guy I was tailing.

I know Vegas gets hot, but show some pride, buddy. Don't dress in orange shorts and a tank top that looked like paisley curtains vomited all over you.

The mugger probably figured he looked tough enough that his wardrobe didn't matter. He should dress for the job he wanted, not the one he had. Assuming he had higher aspirations than petty crime. There are reasons you don't see a lot of senior citizens mugging people.

Still, the one accessory he chose for success was the revolver in his right hand. For most crime victims, that would have been their focus instead of his outfit.

I'm a bit different than most people.

I've also taught a self-defense class or two. All the experts say the same thing—when confronted by a mugger, give them whatever they want. Nothing you own is worth dying for.

Fantastic advice, but I wasn't going to follow it. Being tormented by typical and psychotic bullies as a kid rewired my brain. It's what started me on the path to being a professional MMA fighter. Why I retired too and how I ended up a PI.

Tank Top didn't look nervous. Probably thought he had no reason to be, what with him clocking in at about six foot one while I came in at a whopping five foot six.

Another thing that self-defense experts will tell you is to toss whatever the mugger wants behind them. When they go after it, run the other way screaming fire or something to get people's attention.

Following the first half of that advice, I slowly removed my wallet from my suit jacket like a good little victim, then tossed it underhand to his right side.

Tank Top took the bait and turned to watch my billfold fly by, which was all the opening I needed.

I hit him in the solar plexus, followed by an uppercut to his jaw, then broke his wrist. When I was done, Tank Top was out cold on the sidewalk, his gun in my hand. He'd be hurting when he woke.

I wasn't going to lose any sleep over it. A guy who uses a gun to rob somebody gets zero sympathy from me.

Popping open the revolver's cylinder, I shook all six cartridges onto the ground and put a used coffee cup upside down over them, then wiped off my prints from everything I touched. I wasn't about to set myself up as a suspect in a crime that I had nothing to do with. Particularly since at least one cop I ticked off back when I worked for Clark County Child Protective Services would love to frame me for anything he could.

I placed the gun by Tank Top's side, took his phone out of his pocket, and called 911. I masked my voice using a horrible southern accent with a phony deep voice that sounded like the bass man in an old doo-wop group.

911 does record calls, you know.

I let the operator know the mugger's location and that he was unconscious and needed an ambulance. I made sure to mention the empty gun and cartridges.

After disconnecting the call, I did another fingerprint wipe and dropped the phone onto his chest.

Casually scanning the street, I checked for any pedestrians or looky-loos in the nearby windows. Lucky for me, Tank Top chose a dark part of the street, or somebody might have called the cops on me.

Moving away, I stood at the end of the block watching over Tank Top until I heard the sirens, then casually disappeared around the corner.

CHAPTER TWO

I headed toward a theater that'd been abandoned for a few years. I'd heard that a developer bought the place to knock it down and turn it into condos.

It should have been empty, but apparently, no one had told the crowd streaming in.

Pop-up clubs were a thing. Think raves for people with money.

I was stopped at the door by a guy with lots of muscle and no hair. His head looked like a cue ball.

"Phone?" he asked. He was scanning barcodes on phone screens before letting people in.

"Someone said they'd leave a ticket for me at the window."

Cueball checked his list for the name I gave him, motioned me through a metal detector, then patted me down. He missed some tools of the trade I had hidden in my suit.

Cueball pulled my cell out of my pocket.

"Can I have my phone back, please?"

"Sorry, sir, all phones have to be checked. We don't permit recording in Spot 51." He peeled off a numbered ticket and stuck one end to the back of my phone. He then tore off the other and gave it to me. "Pick it up over there—" He pointed to an old-fashioned coat check room. " —on your way out."

I'd noticed the metal detector inside the foyer during my earlier surveillance which is why I went back to put my gun in my car, but the phone thing threw me. Private investigators such as myself depend on our cell phones, especially on a surveillance job. I debated taking the cell phone back to my car or pressing on without it. I'd already lost sight of my target, Henry Lareau. If I wasted even more time, I could lose him altogether, which would upset his lovely wife, Betty.

Betty wasn't the woman he was spending the evening with. The wife suspected as much, which is why she hired me to tail him and get proof. Cheating invalidated their prenup. Seems in exchange for her agreeing to sign it, Betty insisted on severe financial consequences for cheating. She was going to be a wealthy woman if I could supply evidence of her husband's infidelity.

I'd gotten some shots yesterday of Lareau and his lady friend at a no-tell motel, but they hadn't left the curtains open. All I got was some footage of them going in and coming back out. Plus, some of him being a real class act and not even getting out to open the passenger door of his green Lamborghini when he picked up his date.

Not that she seemed to mind. Or maybe she was just tired because as soon as they started moving, she lay down with her head in his lap and didn't pop up again until they got to the motel. Incriminating, but far from proof.

If I went back to the car, the police could still be on the scene. I didn't want to explain what happened and not make it back. Luckily my phone was one of three surveillance recorders I had.

I took the phone check stub and pressed on to the ticket window.

"I believe you're holding a ticket for Quinton Decker." Not my actual name. I'd followed Lareau to the pop-up club, then checked the place out, looking for the best way in. Back and fire doors were all shut tight. Luckily, I overheard somebody on his phone say he would leave a ticket under that name at the box office.

The kid behind the plexiglass didn't look old enough to drink. Not that I was so many years past twenty-one myself.

He gave me a printed piece of paper with a barcode and nothing else.

"Here you go, Mr. Decker." The kid slid the paper through the window, then stopped. "You're Quinton Decker?"

I smiled. "I don't like to brag."

"Of Stupendous Talent Management, Inc.?"

In my business, sometimes I have to take some big risks, well aware it could work or could blow up in my face. It was still too early to tell how this would work out.

"Who else would I be?"

The kid squinted at me. I didn't have to be a mind reader to realize he was working out if I was lying and, if I was, how far up the Vegas social order I was. Even a medium-sized fish in this desert pond could make a guppy's life a living hell.

"I thought you were much older. And taller."

I tried my best to look embarrassed and whispered. "Junior."

"What'd you call me?"

I shook my head. "I'm Quinton Decker *Junior*. My dad's the big boss at Stupendous—" I leaned forward in a conspiratorial whisper, "—but he's training me to take over."

Kid broke out into a grin. "I get it, Mr. Decker. I have this screenplay, and I was wondering, would you take a look at it?"

I did my best not to chuckle. I wasn't that different from him. He had a screenplay. I had an entire Vegas show scripted out, scored, and choreographed. Not that I'm likely ever to see it performed. Kid was just hoping I was his one-in-a-billion break.

"We rep screenplays from writers we know." No agent worth his salt would get excited over somebody offering them a script while they're out socially. His face fell, and he still hadn't given me the ticket. "But why don't you check out the submissions section on our website?"

The kid's face picked itself up and tried to smile. "I'll do that. Do you mind if I mention that we met?"

"You could, but it won't make much difference. We have people who go through all that before it gets to me. If it's good enough, they'll pass it on."

Kid nodded vigorously. "Gotcha." The ticket slid all the way across, and I grabbed it. "Enjoy the Cryptid Fight Club."

So, this place was an illegal pop-up fight club. There's no fighting in Vegas unless the powers that be get their cut.

Not that these things get busted much without a good reason. Boxing and MMA probably make Vegas billions every year, but some people like their fights more hardcore. Unless someone gets killed, the cops leave operations like this alone if the players are high enough on the food chain.

Cueball scanned the paper, fed it into a shredder, then opened the theater door for me.

CHAPTER THREE

The theater seats had been removed, and there was a good-sized crowd. Once inside, I noticed several boxing-style posters on the wall. They all proclaimed Spot 51 Presents Cryptid Fight Club across the top. One dated last week read Bigfoot vs. Yeti, with drawings of the creatures instead of photos of the fighters. That was odd. Sure, fighters get nicknames, but most want credit, even in an illegal match.

Not wanting to draw attention, I kept moving into the crowd. A waitress in a short skirt and a low top approached me.

"Table service, sir?"

"No, thanks." No reason to spend five hundred bucks for a twenty-five-dollar bottle of booze just to sit at a table ringside. Although the ring was really just a huge cage with two chain-link tunnels that fed into it.

Someone had paid a pretty penny to bring in that much sand for the cage floor. Sand was good at soaking up blood. Fighting to see who's better makes sense to me, but a blood sport to thrill a crowd turned my stomach.

I spotted Lareau. He'd gotten table service. I noticed someone in the back who seemed to have paid for throne service. The guy sat on a high-backed armchair on what had once been the stage. Maybe he paid extra for no lights. All I could make out from his silhouette was he was wearing a suit and had a big head.

Continuing his show of class, Lareau was trying to suck his date's lips off.

I looked his way, so the camera in my glasses got a nice shot, then turned away and pointed the camera in my watch toward the sloppy make-out session.

The glasses looked normal, and the watch had an old-fashioned dial with hands. I ran one or the other constantly. You'd be surprised how many times footage has got me out of trouble.

Take Tank Top the mugger. He could claim I attacked him, but my recording would prove otherwise.

Lareau was kneading his date's derrière like he was making bread.

The woman seemed to enjoy it, but it was that fake kind of happy. She had the looks and curves that would make some men give her surgeon a standing ovation. Add to that her tiny black dress and blonde hair that flowed down below her shoulders, and she was an impressive trophy date.

Anyplace else in the country, a woman built like her would've been considered one of the most beautiful women in town. Here in the land of fantasy, she ranked slightly above average. Oddly, she looked familiar, but I couldn't place her.

It may have been judgmental, but I was thinking sugar baby. Sure, there's the possibility she's actually in love with Lareau, but I doubted it. The guy was no prize, even with a nice haircut, spray-on tan, and a high-end suit to cover up his middle-aged paunch. It'd be very unusual for a woman of her looks to be interested in an older chubby guy at least fifteen years her senior if he was working for minimum wage.

On the plus side, I now had evidence of infidelity, but it would be better for Betty Lareau's case if it were of the more intimate variety.

The show of class continued as he snaked one of his hands beneath the black dress. The blonde slapped the hand away, so it returned to its bread-making motions on the outside of her clothing.

"I know you," a voice said from behind me.

One danger of being undercover is somebody recognizing you.

I've lived in Vegas my whole life, so odds are there will be times I bump into someone who knows me. Put me in fighting circles, and my chances of being recognized jumped exponentially.

Some fight fans consider me a minor celebrity. It makes me uncomfortable, but I do my best to deal with it.

I looked up into a smiling, slightly drunken face but turned my wrist, so it was still recording Lareau.

"I knew it. You're Rufus Griffin! I've followed your MMA career since you first started in the Supreme Fight Federation."

"Thank you very much," I said and tried to move away.

"Rufus... Do you mind if I call you Rufus?" He didn't stop long enough for me to answer. "I was so impressed when you won the SFF welterweight championship and that half-million-dollar purse. If you kept at it, you would have been a millionaire easy. Why don't you fight anymore?"

My fan was not getting the hint that I was trying to get away from him. "Some things are more important than money."

He laughed loud and hard. "I don't know what that would be. Hey, I heard you were raised by showgirls. And that you killed a guy. Any of that true?"

Both were, more or less. Although there was a lot more to the story, fanboy had stumbled across the reason I stopped fighting. It was the latter, not the former.

"You know what, Rufus? You should get in there and fight with these beasts. Now that would be that be something to see!"

"Beasts?" The fights here must be really brutal.

Out of the corner of my eye, I saw Lareau and his date get up and head toward the restrooms.

"It was great meeting you, but I have to see a man about a dog."

I plunged into the standing portion of the crowd.

My fan didn't follow.

CHAPTER FOUR

Lareau and the blonde had almost reached the restrooms while I was still struggling to get out of the crowd. Mr. Class looked down each side of the hallway. Satisfied that no one was watching, he opened the men's room door and led his date inside.

This was good footage. There was no logical reason for him to take a woman into the men's room other than sex, at least not one that any judge was going to believe. I slowed my pace, so they had some time to get started but didn't want to miss the show. Lareau might be a sprinter instead of a marathon man.

I went in, happy the door hadn't been locked from the inside. Smart cheaters do that kind of thing. I eased the door closed quietly. They wouldn't have noticed if I slammed it.

Mr. Class and his date were in the closest of three stalls, the walls of which were higher than his head, although hers bounced just over the top. The room echoed with all the bumping and groaning that one expects in that situation. I crept up to the stall and took my glasses off. Next, I bent down, pointed them upward under the door.

Yeah, it wasn't exactly a classy way to make a living, but taking high-paying jobs like this let me offer a sliding scale for people who needed help and couldn't afford my regular rates.

Next, the glasses went topside, pointing downward at the adulterous couple and held there long enough Mrs. Lareau would have plenty of evidence to convince any judge to throw out her prenup.

I backed away and put the recording glasses back on as an air vent ricocheted off the wall near the ceiling. I startled as the metal clattered to the ground. Then something flew out of the vent, barely a blur.

Outside the men's room, there came the pitter-patter of heavy feet running. "I think it went in here."

I was pretty sure we were about to get visitors, so I ducked in the furthest of the stalls and pulled the door closed as the blur zoomed around the room like some huge hummingbird.

As the door slammed open, the flying creature stilled, perching on the handicapped rail in my stall.

Now that I could see it clearly, I still wasn't quite sure what it was. It was maybe ten inches long with wings and feathers, which normally would make me guess it was a snow-white bird, probably related to an owl. It was the pair of four-inch antlers that threw me off. If it were a deer, it would be a ten-pointer. Its pupils were huge, and its body trembled. I didn't need to be a professional investigator to deduce that this critter was terrified.

Technically, whatever was happening was none of my business. With most people, "technically" often gets in the way of doing the right thing. With my ingrained loathing for bullies, I decided I had to least try to help the little fella get away.

I motioned with my hand as I pulled open my jacket, then whispered, "Come on, I'll try to get you out of here."

If I were under oath, I would have sworn not only did the critter stop trembling but his mouth around his short beak seemed to curl up into a smile.

It didn't climb in my jacket as I suggested. Instead, it fluttered to the floor and gently burrowed into my right trouser cuff, then wrapped its wings around my calf. It flattened itself to the contours of my leg so well that when I looked down, I couldn't make out any bump or bulge.

The first stall got kicked in, causing Lareau's date to screech.

"What the hell are you doing? Do you have any idea who I am?"

"Don't know and don't care," answered a voice with a heavy Brooklyn accent. "Pull your pants up and get your floozy out of here."

"Henry, are you going to let him call me a floozy?" the blonde demanded in a cartoon-like voice, and I remembered where I knew her from. Lareau was either extremely brave or equally stupid to fool around with the girlfriend of the SFF's heavyweight champ.

Lareau didn't seem to be in a rush to get physical with the men. "Now, sweetie…"

"Don't you 'now, sweetie' me. Are you going to let them disrespect me like that?" She screamed. "Get your hands off me!"

"Sorry. We have to frisk you both."

Lareau reprimanded the men, then apparently got frisked himself. I pressed a button on the arm of the recording glasses that rested on my left ear. It triggered a complete video dump of all its footage to my cloud.

The watch needed to be hooked up directly to download. I paid for quality, but somebody might recognize that either one was a recording device and destroy them. The financial loss would hurt, but that's why my client contract included expenses.

The man with the accent gave a halfhearted apology for the floozy comment, so Lareau and his date grumbled and left.

The goons kicked open the middle stall. It was empty.

Rather than wait for the inevitable, I flushed the toilet with my foot, opened the door, and stepped out with my hands up. Flushing the toilet may have seemed unnecessary, but it wasn't. A goon isn't necessarily dumb. I didn't want them to question why it was empty.

"I don't want no trouble. I was just answering nature's call, and I'm happy to leave," I said as meekly as I could, going so far as to hunch my shoulders forward slightly. The intent was that by being so cooperative and harmless looking, these two wouldn't feel the need to do something brutal. I didn't want to blow my cover, but a thousand a day plus expenses wasn't worth taking a beating over. And unlike the mugger, these guys probably knew how to fight. I watched the two men smirk, then exchange a glance.

I moved toward the exit, but the much bigger of the pair stopped me then frisked my chest and pelvic area but didn't bother going down below my knees. I guess the bird was pretty smart not to listen to my plan.

"Nada," said the big man, a real tall drink of water.

"Yo, you see any animals in here?" asked the short one with the thick Brooklyn accent.

I called up my best confused expression. "Like a rat?"

Brooklyn shrugged. "A rat, a bird. Anything at all."

I shook my head. "Nothing like that. There was a big clang. I thought it was the couple." I pretended to notice the uncovered vent for the first time. "Maybe it went out through there?"

"It is pretty smart. The dingbat could have made the noise to draw us in here, then doubled back to get out," Tall Drink said.

Brooklyn looked up at the vent, and I could hear his teeth grind. He turned to me. "You're excused, sir. Go enjoy the fights."

He didn't have to tell me twice.

My first instinct was to head straight for the exit and get me and the bird—which, judging by Tall Drink's slip of the tongue, was called a dingbat—out of there, but I didn't. That might attract the attention of the two goons from the bathroom. After all, who pays big money to see an illegal fight and then leaves before it starts? With no cell phone, I couldn't even fake getting an emergency call.

I turned toward the fight cage and froze. It was worse than I thought. Spot 51 resorted to gimmicks. There was a huge creature at the door to each fence tunnel. One looked like a giant man sloth, maybe eight feet in height. The other appeared to be a seven-foot-tall cross between a praying mantis and a man.

It was sad. Obviously, they weren't real. They'd gotten a couple of down-on-their-luck fighters to play dress up. Maybe they were trying to cash in on the trend for celebrities to go on singing and dancing shows and hide their real identities in costumes. Maybe when it was done, the Rock and Mike Tyson would unmask, but I doubted it. Not that I understood the point of a masked show. Why compete without recognition? It seemed to go against the whole point of wanting to be a celebrity.

A voice boomed over speakers. "Welcome to another night at Spot 51's Cryptid Fight Club."

The club went wild, cheering.

"Our preliminary match this evening features, in the east corner, a beast from the Amazon, Mapinguari! He may look cuddly, but those claws are nothing to laugh at. Take a look at those beautiful natural blades—each one is six inches long and razor-sharp. In the west corner, hailing from the great state of New Jersey, is Mantis Man. Part man, part bug, and all fighter, although he's probably thrilled that there are no females of his kind around. After all, we all know how mating ends for a male praying mantis."

There was laughter and chuckles as the tunnel gates were pulled open.

The costumes were top-notch, and this was coming from a guy who moonlights at a shop that provides the best outfits in Vegas for shows and rentals. These both looked damn real to me, especially the way Mantis Man's arms moved.

The giant sloth and the Mantis Man moved to opposite sides of the cage, neither showing much interest in fighting. Brooklyn and Tall Drink stepped up to the fence, wielding what looked like giant cattle prods.

The goons held the zappers near the costumed fighters. Two zaps lit up the cage, loud enough to be heard throughout the theater.

The crowd was into the idea of these two guys getting jolted, judging by all the whooping and hollering.

My next thought was Spot 51 dealt in human trafficking because sloth-guy started trembling while Mantis Man made a swipe at Tall Drink, stopped only by the chain-link fence. If anyone pulled that crap on me at a match, I'd walk. These guys didn't, which made me think maybe they couldn't.

With obvious reluctance, the fighters carefully inched toward each other. With the padding that had to be on those outfits, things could probably get pretty violent with neither guy taking too much real damage.

Whatever was going on here seemed closer to pro wrestling than MMA. Not to discount the strength and athletic ability of a professional wrestler, but at the end of the day, their fights are choreographed, the outcome of their matches decided before they even start.

The crowd's yelling turned ugly because they weren't getting the violence they'd paid for, so Tall Drink pressed an air horn. Mantis Man startled and lunged forward to swipe at the Mapinguari, who ducked to swipe at the Mantis Man's underbelly with those six-inch claws.

Both fighters screamed in pain, and neither howl sounded human. The cheers of the crowd sadly did.

Sloth guy growled, and Mantis dude's high-pitched screeching sounded like something out of a Godzilla film.

I stared. Red blood oozed out from the giant sloth's back, and some sort of green goo dripped out of the Mantis Man's abdomen. Costumes didn't bleed.

Holy crap! These were actual cryptids!

CHAPTER FIVE

At that moment, I couldn't have turned away if you'd offered me a thousand bucks.

Mantis Man leapt across the cage and landed on top of the Mapinguari. Its scythe-like arms slashed toward the furry neck.

The giant sloth reached back, grabbed onto the giant insect's head, and flipped the huge bug over.

What followed was a flurry of limbs as the pair went at it with all the gusto of a couple of gladiators who knew it was kill or be killed.

I stared until I felt a tug on my leg. I'd forgotten about my feathered stowaway. The dingbat's head peaked out upside down from my pant leg. Its beak tugged on my cuff.

It took me a second to realize he was trying to get me moving. I let his pulling guide me back past the restrooms, then around the corner toward what was once the theater's dressing rooms.

Seeming to swivel his head almost a full three hundred and sixty degrees, the dingbat checked all around us then dropped out of my cuff to hover in front of a door, which he pointed at with his antlers.

"You want me to go in there?"

I felt rather silly and didn't expect an answer, but the dingbat nodded his head up and down.

"Look, I have no idea what's going on here, but I'm not looking to do any breaking and entering."

Faster than I could blink, the dingbat shot down to grab hold of my suit sleeve with its talons, then yanked my arm up and dropped my hand on the doorknob.

The feathered guy's eyes seemed to swell as his beak somehow contorted into a frown.

Maybe I'm a sucker, but I couldn't say no. I tried the knob, and to nobody's surprise, it didn't move.

The dingbat frantically shot back and forth between me and the door, hovering better than any hummingbird.

I pointed out the obvious. "It's locked." The bird gave me another sad look. "What do you want me to do?"

The bird answered by landing on my shoulder. To my surprise, he flapped his wings with enough force to yank me forward.

"Me going through those doors is important?" He hovered and nodded his head. "Did Timmy fall down the well?"

The bird sort of tilted his head and squinted. Okay, it understood English, but not so strong on cultural references. "Is there somebody back there in trouble, someone who needs help?"

The bird nodded so frantically that his entire body rocked back and forth.

I took a deep breath and shook my head. I glanced back over my shoulder. There was nobody in the corridor.

The door had no deadbolt, but it wasn't going to be opened by sliding a credit card along the jamb.

I'd been searched for weapons, but they weren't looking for lock picks, which I'd hidden in a narrow tube of material along the bottom of my suit coat. I pulled open the Velcro on each side and slid out a pair of flexible lock-pick tools. Even in Vegas, it's illegal for a private investigator to carry them, which is why I also have a locksmith license. I can still be charged for picking a lock, but not for having the tools on my person.

The lock wasn't complicated. I had it open in less than a minute.

I pulled open the door, using my sleeve to avoid leaving fingerprints. The room was dark. Since I hadn't planned to do a break-in, I didn't pack a flashlight or gloves, and my cell was still in the phone check. The air vibrated as the dingbat flew over my head through the small gap of the cracked open door. With a last look behind, I slid in after him, locking the door from the inside. I made a cursory fingerprint wipe but didn't think these guys were likely to call the police.

There were no windows, and the only light shone in around the door. Squatting, I covered my eyes for a minute, giving them a chance to adjust to the darkness and making myself a smaller target in case anyone wanted to take a shot at me.

By the time I uncovered my eyes, I'd noticed a stench reminiscent of a barn or maybe a zoo.

Standing, I stepped forward only to jump back when something big and metal shook. I bumped into something, then realized it was a vanity table. I fumbled around until I found the switch to turn on the lights around the mirror, hoping nobody outside would notice.

I screamed, but the bird covered my mouth with his wing, muffling the sound.

There in front of me stood a big blue gorilla. I tried to back away, but I was already against the vanity, which was against the wall.

The blue ape growled at me.

Double-checking that the cage was locked, I whispered, "I ain't scared of you."

I think even the gorilla knew I was lying.

The dingbat hovered between us and made lots of different hooting noises. The blue ape responded with grunting noises of his own, then calmed down and nodded at me. I nodded back. It seemed polite, and I figured maybe it would help hide the fact that I was freaked out.

The blue guy's eyes were red, but not like a scary monster. More like bloodshot from crying.

Damn it. This was another cryptid waiting to be thrown into that fight cage against its will.

The dingbat flew between the bars, landing on the blue ape's chest. He wrapped his wings around the blue neck, and the ape gently wrapped his hands around the bird.

For crying out loud. They were hugging. The dingbat had dragged me back here to rescue his friend the...

What the heck was he? A blue bigfoot? His head looked a bit ape-like with a touch of wolf in there. His large ears looked like they had come from an elf, their pointed tips rising up over the sides of his head. He had some seriously large teeth.

The dingbat came back through the bars to hover by my face. Like before, he lifted my arm by my suit cuff and dropped my hand on the cage lock.

This wasn't as simple as the door. The bars looked thick enough to hold an elephant, and the lock was huge.

"My picks are too small to open that," I said, but it didn't matter to the dingbat. He just wanted to free his friend.

Was that even a good idea? I was against any kind of animal fighting, be it dogs or roosters or I guess even cryptids. But would I be doing more harm than good, letting the blue bigfoot out of the cage? It was an extremely large wild animal, one I was entirely unfamiliar with. Would it attack people? Would it go after me?

It probably weighed three times what I did and topped out at seven feet tall. Without a large-caliber rifle, tranquilizer darts, or maybe a small truck, there was no way I was going to be able to stop this thing.

If it went after people, any injuries or deaths would be on my conscience. Even if it didn't, a cop's reaction to seeing something like that in downtown Vegas would be to shoot it. I didn't want that to happen either.

The dingbat grew more frantic as it darted about through the air.

"I understand you want me to let your friend out, but how do I know it's not going to hurt anybody?"

As if in answer, the blue bigfoot sat on the ground and shook his head. I guess the bird wasn't the only creature who understood English. Then a pair of giant bat wings wrapped around the creature. Was there a bat cryptid attacking him from behind?

It was no attack. The wings belonged to big blue. My mind flashed back to some other posters that I'd glanced at for a fight tonight and tomorrow night.

"So, you're a batsquatch." The blue guy nodded. "Look, I understand you don't want to be here. What's going on out there is all kinds of wrong, but you're huge, and I don't know you. How do I know you're not going to hurt someone?"

The batsquatch stood up slowly, pointed one finger at his chest, shook his head, and then lifted his arms like a boxer.

"You don't want to fight?" The batsquatch nodded.

It was clear I wasn't dealing with a beast, but an intelligent creature who just happened to be something other than human. My entire life's philosophy was based on standing up for the little guy. Despite his size, the batsquatch was the little guy in this situation. I couldn't leave him.

"You promise you won't hurt any innocent people?"

The batsquatch nodded.

I let out a long breath. "Fine. I'll get you out of here and figure out what to do with you after. I'm Rufus Griffin. Do you two have names?"

The dingbat hooted like an owl several times.

"Hootie?" The bird with antlers nodded. "How about you, big guy?"

What followed was a cacophony of grunts and clicks. "There's no way I'd be able to repeat that. How about something resembling a human name?"

The batsquatch pointed to a TV in the corner and brought his arm up in front of the lower part of his face with his wing resting on his arm.

"Dracula?"

The blue furry guy shook his head and stood in a heroic pose with his hands on his hips, his shoulders back, and his chest puffed up. His wings wrapped around him like a cape, and his long-pointed ears perked up straighter. "Batman?"

His blue furry face lit up in a smile. At least, I hoped it was a smile.

"That one's already taken, but he has another name. How about Wayne?"

The batsquatch gave me a thumbs up.

"All right, Wayne and Hootie, help me figure out how to get this unlocked."

As I examined the lock, I sensed Hootie flying behind me. The drawer on the vanity slid open, and then the dingbat hovered in front of me, holding a keyring.

"You know, if you had keys, Wayne could've put them in and turned the lock himself."

Wayne shook his head and tried to stick his hand through the bars. It didn't fit.

"I stand corrected." I put the key in the lock and turned it. The metal door popped open.

I had to resist tensing. Although I'd helped with the jailbreak, I hadn't forgotten the danger involved if the batsquatch lashed out at me.

Wayne didn't. He stepped out of the cage and followed me toward the door. I opened it to peek out. There was no one in the side corridor, but I could hear the crowd cheering for the cryptid fight going on. With no windows in the dressing room, the only way out was going back the way we came in.

It couldn't be that easy, could it?

CHAPTER SIX

I shut the door, searching the dressing room for something a batsquatch might be able to wear. There wasn't much hope of him passing as a human, but maybe there was something here that could hide the fact that he looked like the child of Cookie Monster and a giant bat.

A white tarp covered something in the corner. I pulled it off and found a bunch of boxes filled with clothes. Sadly, the outfits were skimpy and designed for women who fell in the size zero-to-four range, none of which would cover more than a single limb on the big guy.

But maybe that could be enough.

Before her disappearance, my mother had been one of the more renowned Las Vegas showgirls. My sister Amber and I had spent most of our childhood backstage or in empty auditoriums while she rehearsed for shows. The average showgirl costume weighed around forty to sixty pounds and cost a small fortune. Despite that, wardrobe malfunctions and issues were commonplace and sometimes had to be fixed instantly as there was no time for a seamstress to do anything. You'd be amazed at the uses I've seen for duct tape.

I dumped clothes on the floor and, sure enough, found a roll of duct tape. I picked up a matching pair of white tops and brought them over to Wayne. "Hold your arms up while I see what kind of disguise I can rig up."

I pulled the shirts up on his arms, then went around behind them to duct tape them together across his shoulders, making sure to use a top and bottom layer so it wouldn't stick to any blue fur.

To my delight, the shirts stayed on and could pass as sleeves if drunken hobo chic was actually a thing.

"Hootie, bring that tarp over and help me wrap it around Wayne."

The tarp was the cloth kind painters used. It was dusty and stained but was bigger than a king-size sheet. The dingbat flapped his wings and dropped the tarp over Wayne's shoulders and wings. I pulled it so it looked even and duct-taped the edges together from the inside over his right shoulder, making a toga. A bad toga that my Aunt Lizzie, a retired showgirl-turned-costumer, would've been embarrassed by, but I wasn't trying to win any fashion shows.

Hootie floated over to me with three more white shirts. I connected each to one of the arm shirts Wayne was already wearing, so material now went down past his furry fingertips. I used the third to cover his left shoulder.

Even with Wayne's wings tucked along his back and sides so they were covered by the tarp, the batsquatch looked like a shower curtain that had learned to walk.

I picked one last thing from the mess I dumped from the boxes and held it up.

"And now for the *pièce de résistance*," I said and motioned Wayne to bend down. I placed a bad blonde wig on top of the batsquatch's head. It was supposed to be shoulder-length hair, but on this cryptid's oversized head, it barely covered the sides of his neck. I pulled a lot of hair forward to cover his face.

In a well-lit room, the disguise wouldn't fool anybody. Fortunately, Spot 51, like most clubs, was dimly lit.

"Anybody looking at you will quickly realize that you're not a seven-foot-tall woman, so I need you to follow me closely and don't stop moving. You understand?"

I expected a nod but instead got a salute. How much TV had the batsquatch watched?

I cracked open the door again. While the coast to the exit wasn't clear, there was no one in the corridor.

I turned back and whispered, "Showtime."

CHAPTER SEVEN

The dingbat disappeared beneath the painter's tarp toga. I stepped out first, and the batsquatch followed. Wayne held his legs and feet far apart and kind of lurched his body sideways with each step while bent forward. Considering his body shape, I guess I shouldn't have been too surprised he moved more like a gorilla than a human.

I learned long ago that the best way to get noticed is to act like you're sneaking around. I always act like I belong wherever I am, whether I do or not.

Unfortunately, I didn't have the time to teach that skill set to a seven-foot-tall blue cryptid with bat wings, so I just had to be extremely impressive in demonstrating how much I belonged to compensate for my huge, ape walking, blonde companion in a toga.

We turned the corner and strolled past the bathrooms just as a drunk stepped out of the men's room.

He looked up at the giant blonde, blinked a few times, then rubbed his eyes. We didn't stick around to find out what he did next.

In seconds, we came out on the main floor and kept moving. When we were almost a third of the way to the main exit, I thanked my lucky stars because it looked like we were going to make it.

Which, of course, is when the hollering crowd went wild. I dared to look at the ring just as the Mantis Man flung the giant sloth high enough that he hit the chain-link ceiling and crashed down onto the sand. The Mapinguari was down for the count, but it looked like it was still breathing. As the Mantis Man advanced on its fallen opponent, four guys ran out into the cage, acting a lot like rodeo clowns. Only instead of makeup and crazy clothes, they were dressed in helmets and full body armor. They got between the two cryptids holding those six-foot-long cattle prods. Mantis Man wasn't too impressed and swung at one of them with his uninjured scythe-like arm.

The guy in the armor suit screamed and slammed into the chain-link fence. Two of the other armored clowns moved between him and the cryptid, zapping the Mantis Man's underside.

The green cryptid convulsed and fell to the sand. The three remaining armored clowns twisted something on the handle of each of their prods, which then emitted a much louder zapping noise. Mantis Man rose to his legs and backed into his tunnel.

As the huge bug disappeared into its enclosure, the three armored clowns followed, leading with their zappers.

Next, a brown-haired woman in a white lab coat ran out onto the field and tended to the giant sloth. The battered and fallen armored clown was left to lie where he landed. I guess he wasn't worth as much as one of the evening's main attractions.

By that point, we were maybe thirty feet from the door when someone finally noticed us.

Another drunk shouted, "That's got to be the biggest, ugliest woman I've ever seen."

We didn't stop, but the drunk's comment drew security's attention. Cueball the doorman and a friend, almost as large and chemically enhanced, got between us and the exit. The musclebound pair held their hands up like a pair of synchronized crossing guards.

The second 'roider's nose had been broken more than once, and it looked like something had nibbled off parts of his right ear. From his looks, I'd guess he'd done some boxing.

"Where you think you're going?" Cueball asked. Nibbles fell in behind him but off to the side.

"Fight's over. Figured I'd beat the traffic."

"We got more fights on the bill tonight. That was only the first of three." Cueball looked up at the poorly disguised batsquatch. "What exactly are you supposed to be?"

"That's no way to talk to a lady," I said.

Cueball gave me an incredulous glance. "No way a woman is that big."

"Who are you to judge and disagree if someone says they're a woman? Someone who works with the public should show better manners."

Cueball looked down in an attempt to intimidate me and couldn't figure out why it wasn't working.

I tried not to smile. It's amazing how often guys who acted tough bought into their own hype. Cueball balled his right hand and bent his elbow, bringing his fist level with my chest. "This here's my manners. Want to see how good they are?"

Cueball had taken so many steroids that he couldn't even bring his elbow down to his side. Sure, he could bench press me and probably any friend I cared to bring, but his bulk limited his range.

I took a step back, so I'd be out of reach if he decided to swing. If that fist managed to connect with my head, I'd be loopy long enough for him and his pal to kick the brown and squishy right out of me.

"I suppose we can do without the etiquette lessons this evening. Now, if you'll just step aside, my friend and I will get out of your hair." Okay, it was a stupid and cheap shot, but it felt good, even if I had to fight hard to hide a smirk.

"Not yet. Something's not right here. I don't remember letting anyone her size in tonight. What about you, Reggie?" I guess that was Nibbles' real name.

He shook his head. "I most certainly did not. I would remember meeting such a... statuesque woman. So, you couldn't afford tickets and somehow found another way in and thought you could stiff CFC—" Cryptid Fight Club, I guessed. "—out of its hard-earned money?"

"We would never consider doing such a thing. Your partner checked me in."

Cueball squinted at me. "Yeah, I did, but if neither of us checked her in, she didn't use a ticket to gain entry."

"Fine, if you don't believe us, kick us out," I suggested.

Nibbles shook his head again. "Can't do that. Sets a terrible example for other would-be gatecrashers."

"Fine, if you going to be that way, we'll buy another ticket." I carried around five hundred dollars in emergency cash for just such situations. "What's the damage?"

"Three grand," Cueball said.

I tried not to choke as I swallowed my own spit. Even with the regular cash in my wallet, I didn't have a third of that.

I pulled the five hundred out of my pocket and held it in front of me. "This is all the cash I have on me right now. How about you take this as a down payment, and I'll come back with the rest."

I didn't think they'd buy it, so I wasn't disappointed when Nibbles shook his head.

"I'm afraid that just won't do. Not by a longshot. You're going to have to come up with a lot more real quick."

I pulled out my wallet and added the bills to what was already in my hand.

"That makes seven hundred and twenty dollars. I don't have anymore."

Nibbles grinned the type of smile that would frighten small children and lots of adults.

"Seems unlikely you would bring that little to bet with. Mind if we search you?"

"I mind, but your search isn't going to find anything more than this."

"What about the lady?" Cueball asked.

"I'm afraid she left her purse at home." I put the money and the wallet in my pocket so my hands would be free.

Cueball took a step forward. I took another step back. Wayne didn't move.

"How about you let the lady talk for herself," Nibbles said.

"She's got a bad case of laryngitis. Everything she says comes out like a growl. She's a bit embarrassed," I said.

"The only thing you have to be truly embarrassed by is sneaking in. The question is, which of you do we hold on to while the other gets our money?" Nibbles said.

"Keep me," I said. "While she goes to get the cash."

The batsquatch in terrible drag turned and looked down at me in shock. Wayne shook his head.

"It's okay." It was anything but. It wouldn't take these guys long to figure out Wayne wasn't coming back. Then the moment that someone realized the batsquatch was missing, these guys would put two and two together, and my goose would be deep-fried.

Cueball looked back and forth between Wayne and me. "I don't think so. Judging by the way she's dressed, this lady here doesn't have two cents to rub together. I think we're more likely to see our money if we send you to get it while she stays here."

This was going to hell in a handbasket much faster than I had expected. Too bad I hadn't taken the time to stretch and warm up before I came in.

"That's not going to work for me. Either let us go or call the cops. If you don't do either, you're holding us against our will, which, depending on the mood of the district attorney, will get you charged with false imprisonment or unlawful restraint. Maybe both. And that would force me to engage in self-defense of me and my friend."

Cueball laughed, but Nibbles narrowed his eyes.

"We ain't calling nobody. Instead, we're going to take *both* of you in the back so our beating the crap out of you doesn't disturb the paying customers."

Cueball grabbed hold of my left shoulder, expecting to overpower me. He probably would have if I'd been foolish enough to stay still. Instead, I spun in the same direction he'd pulled my shoulder, throwing him off balance as I put all my weight into a punch that smashed into his solar plexus.

My left hand slammed into his kidney as his fist connected with my face, smashing my surveillance glasses to pieces. I responded by punching with the palm of my right hand under his jaw with enough force that the impact knocked him cold. Perfect move for a guy my size when I'm in too close.

I looked at Wayne and then pointed toward the door. "Go. I'll catch up outside."

It was obvious the batsquatch didn't want to leave me. There was no sense in both of us being screwed. I figured I had the better shot of getting out on my own. I always checked in, so my people had an idea of where I was. Plus, the GPS tracker in my watch would be helpful if they came looking for me.

Wayne took some huge strides heading for the door, probably covering twice the distance a human would've in the same number of steps.

Nibbles moved to intercept. I blocked him.

Unlike Cueball, Nibbles didn't waste his time talking or trying to get physical with me. He pulled out a Taser and shot at my chest. I hit the floor like I was doing a leg sweep. Nibbles was too far away for me to touch him but making contact wasn't the point. Dodging the barbs from the Taser was.

The wires landed on top of me. Pulling my hand inside my sleeve, I grabbed them and snapped back to my feet, swinging my arm in a circle. Snapping my wrist, I wrapped the wires around Nibbles's neck. I did it again, then yanked him forward.

My elbow met his nose and my heel, his shin. Neither blow was debilitating but caused sharp pain that would distract all but the most dedicated fighter. It gave me enough time to get close enough to pull the Taser's trigger.

Current coursed through the wires, making Nibbles convulse, twitch, and yell.

I pulled it again. Nibble's limbs shook some more, and he hit the ground.

I sprinted for the door.

Chapter Eight

I was convinced I was going to make it until lightning struck me between my shoulder blades, and it was my turn to hit the ground screaming.

I twisted as I fell. Tall Drink stood over me holding one of those elephant-sized electric prods.

My entire body felt like a bowl of gelatin, and I could barely move. These were the times motor memory comes in handy.

It wasn't fast, and it wasn't pretty, but I got back on my feet.

"You're tougher than you look. That voltage made the Mantis Man curl up into a ball and whimper."

"You're a big shot with that toy in your hand." He was big regardless. "Why don't you put it down and fight me like a man?"

Tall Drink chuckled. "That'd be fighting like an idiot. You just took out two of our strongest guys, neither of which is a push-over. I'm not dumb enough to give up my advantage. How about you just kneel down on the floor there and hook your hands behind your head, and this will all go a lot easier."

"Not unless you flash a badge," I spat back, but the effort made me lightheaded, and I wobbled to one side.

Tall Drink shrugged. "Suit yourself. There ain't no way you're going to be upright after another jolt."

He was probably right. My sluggish muscles weren't up to dodging as he thrust the electric prod toward my chest. I heard the zap, even saw the flicker from the sparks, but I didn't feel any shock.

My eyes dropped toward my chest just in time to see the dingbat plummet to the floor. Hootie got himself between me and Tall Drink, taking the zap meant for me.

Seeing what he'd done to the poor, brave dingbat, I yelled, "You son of a bitch!"

It didn't faze him in the least.

"Looks like I got me a twofer. A troublemaker and our missing dingbat." Tall Drink pointed the giant zapper at me and made some sparks dance on the end of his metal stick. "And still plenty of juice to lay you out."

Dammit if he wasn't right.

I heard the gentle sound of flapping above me. Wayne dive-bombed the goon, and suddenly Tall Drink went airborne. I give the scumbag credit. He didn't scream as he was plucked off the ground by a bat-squatch in women's clothes. Instead, he jabbed his electric prod at the blue abdomen above him and zapped the furry blue flyer.

It was a stupid move to attack what was holding you up in the air. At the jolt, Wayne screamed and glared at Tall Drink. He didn't just drop the guy. He hurled him at the ground.

I couldn't tell how bad Wayne was hurt, but he was still airborne. I bent and picked up Hootie, fearing the worst. He took an awful big zap for such a little creature. I let out a breath I didn't realize I was holding. His chest was moving up and down.

I turned and headed toward the door, but I was slow. Instead of a sprint, I moved like a wounded orangutan trying to tango in six-inch heels.

I didn't have to move under my own power for long.

He wasn't anywhere near as fast as Hootie, but I only saw Wayne drop an instant before he grabbed under my shoulders and lifted me into the air. His wings flapped as we headed for the exit, people fleeing beneath us.

This stupid, crazy plan was working.

At least until it wasn't. From out of nowhere, a weighted net wrapped around us, and we plummeted to the floor.

I figured that was it for me. I guesstimated Wayne's weight in the neighborhood of five hundred pounds. That was a neighborhood you weren't walking away from when it crashed down on top of you. But I didn't die. Wayne twisted his body, purposely taking the brunt of the impact, cushioning my fall.

I tried to squeeze out before I even caught my breath. The strands of the net were too close together for me to even stick a finger through.

Wayne realized what I was doing and used his arms, legs, and wings to stretch the net out to the sides.

It was tangled on the bottom, but there was a gap wide enough for me to push Hootie through and squeeze out after.

I got to my feet. I'd always thought a net was a stupid way to catch somebody. After all, couldn't they just pull it off and get out? The answer to that is no. I tried to get the net off the batsquatch, but it was too tangled for my efforts to do any good. Which is when I noticed Brooklyn put down what looked like a T-shirt cannon and pick up another huge electric prod.

Wayne growled, motioning with his arms for me to go away. He pointed to the door.

"I can't just go..."

Wayne kicked in my direction and pointed at Hootie. He needed me to save his friend, which I could do. I couldn't save him. If I stayed, Hootie and I would be captured too.

It was the hardest kind of math, but I knew the best answer, even if it was still a pretty terrible outcome.

I nodded to the batsquatch, then picked Hootie up off the ground and managed to run. Maybe the adrenaline from the fall and fear of getting caught undid some of the damage from the zap.

As I cleared the door, I didn't stop moving, but I did look back. Somehow, the netted batsquatch was on his feet, his blonde wig fallen off, blocking Brooklyn from chasing me.

I turned away, unable to watch the goon turn the prod on Wayne.

That zap followed by the batsquatch's screams would haunt my nightmares.

Chapter Nine

I'm in pretty good shape. Nothing like when I was fighting, but I still run at least five miles most days. Under normal circumstances, I would've taken off in the opposite direction of my car, hoping to lay a false trail and sneak back once I'd gotten far enough ahead.

The adrenaline boost was wearing off. After practically being electrocuted, I was lucky I was upright and able to see straight. I was doing my best to go the distance, but with the way I felt, that distance needed to be as short as possible.

I sprinted left out of the building and down the street, trying to get further ahead so they couldn't figure out which way I'd run.

As I turned the corner, I saw Brooklyn with a crowd of guys exit the club, stripping off body armor as they ran.

I poured on the speed but tripped over a crack in the sidewalk. Somehow, I didn't hit the ground, but the stumble slowed me down.

Most people assume fighters only think a move or three ahead, but nothing could be further from the truth. We plan for more than a dozen down the line, and a fight was much harder to plot out than chess. For one thing, in traditional chess, there wasn't the worry of one player trying to knock the other person out between moves. For another, every move you make builds on what you did before with some consideration for your opponent's countermoves.

A fight, at least if it's going well, could work out that way, but make the wrong move or allow your opponent to make one for you, and a fight you were winning becomes one you lose.

I hit a button on my key fob. Three cars ahead of me, my trunk silently popped open. I've always watched thriller movies with a critical eye, constantly amazed by how stupid supposedly smart spies and PIs are. A cell phone ring or the beep of a car unlocking gives them away.

Believe it or not, I've planned for this contingency. Not specifically for tonight, but getting away from opponents that outnumber me. When I started doing this for a living, I trained the same way I did for fights, imagining every scenario I might run into and preparing for them.

It wasn't cheap, but those plans I put in place have saved my life on more than one occasion.

I was hoping it would do it again.

My car is modified so when I hit that button, the car doesn't make a sound or flash any lights.

Crouching low on the street side, I crept to the back of my car. Lifting the now-open trunk lid as little as possible, I squeezed inside and slowly closed it on myself. Part of the mods minimized any noise the trunk and doors made when they shut.

Still, the click of the trunk locking seemed as loud as a firecracker. I squeezed toward the back and gently placed Hootie on some rags, then pulled on a Kevlar vest with ceramic plating and a bulletproof army-surplus helmet.

Not that I was planning on confronting anybody. I was pretty sure I saw guns in my pursuers' hands. For the mainstream population, I'm a damn good fighter. As far as being a gunman goes, I can point and pull the trigger, but beyond that, I was nothing special.

My previous investigative experience was in Child and Adult Protective Services. We weren't trained in or allowed to carry weapons. Still, if these guys figured out where I was hiding, it wouldn't hurt to be armed. I kept a few weapons in the trunk. One was a Remington 870 shotgun with an 18.5-inch barrel, so it barely skirted a Nevada law meant to outlaw sawed-off shotguns. The other was a Glock 19. I loaded both. The Glock held more rounds, but the buckshot shells in the Remington would give a wider spray, which meant I was more likely to hit something. It was the better choice if the trunk opened.

Here's hoping it wouldn't come to that.

CHAPTER TEN

I don't care how tough you are. It's pretty damn terrifying hiding in the dark listening for the footsteps of people who want to kill you.

I soon heard the rapid staccato of dress shoes hitting pavement, but that slowed and softened.

"Did anyone see where he went?" I recognized Brooklyn's overly stereotypical accent. A bunch of rapid-fire no's answered him. I couldn't tell for sure, but it sounded like six or seven guys answering.

"You three, search this block. The rest of us will keep looking. Remember, Mr. Cabeza will not be happy if this guy escapes with the dingbat. It's got a match with the tripodero tomorrow."

"That long-legged thing with the big snout and the enormous tail? That one gives me the creeps," came a higher-pitched man's voice.

Laughter followed. "Just that one gives you the creeps?"

"It shot out Alan's eye with a booger bullet and then tried to eat him."

"That's the exact creep factor that will make people pay to watch the fight. Stop yapping and find this moron," Brooklyn ordered.

As the conversation ended, I lay there with the shotgun in one hand and the other resting on the little bird guy. Helluva thing he did, diving in front of the electric prod like that.

I don't know many humans who would've done that for me. At least, Hootie was still breathing.

While I hoped he woke soon, the practical side of me prayed he'd wait until we got out of here. Him waking up suddenly and trying to fly would be bad. If those goons were anywhere nearby, they'd hear the noise, and our gooses—or maybe dingbats—would be barbequed.

Maybe if we managed to stay quiet, we'd avoid the grill entirely.

I didn't move for forty minutes and hadn't heard anything for over twenty. It was time to get out of here. Driving myself would be idiotic. These goons would be watching every car that goes by. If they saw me, I have no doubt they'd shoot first and drag my body out later. Not that it'd be all that easy for them. I didn't have quite enough money to armor my car fully, but I did a favor for a guy who does custom work. He installed bulletproof windows and a windshield at cost. I added some homemade armor plating in the trunk and around the doors and engine, but I'm not sure how effective it would be. It's too expensive to shoot my own car to test it.

Of course, none of that would protect the tires. A few well-placed shots and I'd be stuck. It's not exactly difficult to get a few gallons of gas to pour over the top and add a lit match.

Luckily, I not only planned for this but had used the plan on more than one occasion.

It had to be closing in on one in the morning, but I couldn't tell for sure. The zap had fried my watch. So much for that footage.

Amber was going to be pissed, but I didn't have a choice. Eventually, everybody at Spot 51 and the surrounding clubs would leave and go home. My car being the only one left on the block would be suspicious. It's not exactly hard to trace someone from their license plate, and I wanted to keep these guys from figuring out who I was.

There was a minor hurdle to get over first. My backup cell phone was locked in my glove compartment. Club 51 wasn't giving mine back, which is why I use cheap burner phones and pay for cloud service.

To get to the phone, I had to lower one of the back seats — another custom modification — and crawl through the car to the front seat, retrieve the phone from the glove compartment, and crawl back into the trunk, all without being seen.

No guts, no glory.

Taking the Glock 19, I moved stealthily to the front of the car — at least for me. I'm a fighter, not a ninja. After what seemed like an eternity, I made it back to my hidey-hole and pulled the seatback up behind me.

I turned on the cell and pressed number one on my favorites. Five rings later, Amber picked up with a string of curses that would have made a busted gambler blush in shame.

"How you doing, sis?"

"You call me at 1:12 in the morning to ask me how I'm doing? I'm doing a heck of a lot better than you're going to be when I get a hold of you, Rufus Griffin. You better be dying. Otherwise, I'm going to kill you."

"Not yet, but the odds are getting more likely."

My sister sighed. A good sign. If she'd yelled again and hung up, I'd be up the creek without a boat.

"What happened? The husband you were following spot you and pull a gun?"

"Nope. Got everything I needed on him." At least, I hope I did. I pulled the phone away from my face and checked my cloud. *Yes!* The video files had successfully uploaded. "The problem was the pop-up club they went to. The place was..." How to explain what was happening without sounding like a lunatic? "...fighting animals. I tried to get a couple out but only managed to rescue one. A bunch of seriously bad guys with guns are roaming up and down the streets looking to put some holes in me that I neither want nor need."

There was another sigh. "You're too softhearted for your own good. You almost got yourself killed over two animals? You couldn't have just called the cops?"

"No, I couldn't."

"Shall I assume you're hiding in your trunk, clutching your shotgun like a teddy bear?"

"You shall indeed."

"Let me call Tiffany —" I ran security for a small casino. Well, not the entire casino, just the show areas. Tiffany did most of the actual work. Her contract included a clause that she was expected to help me out when needed. Sadly, that happened a lot more than I'd like. " — and we'll come get you. Figure an hour and fifteen minutes tops."

It was my turn to sigh. "You don't think you can get here a little faster than that?"

She laughed. "Not on your life, brother dear. We're supposed to act like girls coming back to our car after a night of clubbing. Without my hair and makeup done, ain't no one going to buy what you want me to sell. We'll get there when we get there, and you'll thank us for it."

"You're absolutely right. Don't dawdle."

"Just stay safe until then."

"Hopefully even longer than that."

Chapter Eleven

I split my time in the dark between stroking Hootie's feathers, hoping the little guy was okay and listening for footsteps I wanted to hear instead of those I didn't. It wouldn't be hard to tell them apart. The ones I did would undoubtedly be wearing high heels.

An hour and twenty-two minutes after I called, I finally heard two women laughing rambunctiously, sounding for all the world both happy and tipsy. The voices preceded the clickity-clack of their high heels.

It turns out my paranoia was well-founded. At this time of night, or rather morning, the street should be deserted, yet a male voice rang out.

"Good evening, ladies. Looks like you had a good time... No reason for it to end. How about we keep the party going back at my place?"

"No, thanks. We're good," Tiffany said.

It is amazing how much his intentions carried in the man's throaty chuckle. "So, are you two together? That's fine with me. I've always been of the mind that more is merrier. I'm happy to provide a little variety for you or just watch."

"While we thank you for your generous and deviant offer, I'm afraid we'll have to decline," my sister said. "We both just got out of terrible relationships and promised ourselves this would be a girls-only night. We made a vow, and we can't go back on that."

"Totally understandable, though I would like to assure you that I'm deviant in the most wholesome of ways. Perhaps I can get your digits and call you at a time that wouldn't violate any... vows."

"It's been my experience that it's best not to have any prolonged contact with men I meet on dark, deserted streets. You understand," Amber said.

"I can't claim not to be disappointed, but that does seem like a sound policy."

"What are you even doing standing in the shadows where no one can see you?" Tiffany asked. "More than a little creepy, especially if you intend to pick up women."

The man chuckled again. "Excellent point. I wasn't out here looking for a date, but when I saw two women as beautiful as you, I had to take a shot."

"So, if not a date, what are you out here looking for? Do I need to call the cops to protect the next woman who walks down this street?" Tiffany asked.

"Nah, nothing like that. I'm working. My boss is looking for a guy. This guy might be lost, so he sent me and some coworkers out to see if we could help him find his way. He's short, yay tall, blue suit, and brown hair. You wouldn't happen to have seen anyone fitting that description around here?"

I imagined both of them shrugging.

"Not outside, but he could've been one of the guys hitting on us in the club," Amber said.

"That's too bad. The quicker somebody finds this guy, the quicker I get to clock out. Get home safe, ladies."

"Thanks," they replied in unison.

A moment later, the car sank as the ladies got in. We pulled away and drove at least a block before Amber said, "You okay back there, little brother?"

I hate when she refers to me like that, although it's doubly true. Amber's four inches taller and two years older than I am. It's always been fairly obvious to us that our genetic makeup wasn't exactly the same, but Mom's genes were strong enough that we still look alike. We have no idea if we share the same father or not. Mom was notoriously tight-lipped about her love life. That and she disappeared without a trace back when we were in high school, so it's not like we're going to find out anytime soon.

"I'm fine, but my little friend, not so much."

"Assuming you haven't suddenly gone crude on us and that line isn't a euphemism, do you really have an animal back there with you?" Tiffany said.

"No euphemism. He is a very unusual animal and got hurt saving my bacon."

"What is he? Pitbull?"

"Probably safest not to show you while you're driving."

Tiffany always drives. Sometimes to the dismay of her passengers. Unlike Amber, Tiff won't give me grief outright, but I knew darn well that she was taking turns a lot sharper than she needed to just to throw me around the trunk a bit. It took some effort to cushion Hootie from the rough ride. I much prefer complaining over passive-aggressiveness.

"Safe to come out yet?"

"Nope," Tiffany said.

"We're still seeing random guys standing on the street, doing nothing but looking around," Amber said. "The guy who hit on us sounded like he was looking for you."

"He had a gun in a holster under his jacket, so it seems like you made the right call," Tiffany said.

"Was there ever any doubt?"

"When it comes to most of your life, absolutely," Tiffany said, making another turn a lot sharper than she needed to. "When it comes to your job, not usually. Rufus, what the heck is going on?"

Tiffany couldn't take her eyes off the dingbat. "Are you sure someone didn't just glue antlers on a white owl?"

The three of us stood over Hootie, who we'd laid on Aunt Lizzie's workbench in the back of the shop, Exquizite Costumes and Showgirl Accessories.

The workroom seemed a safer idea than the front counter, where we could be seen from the street, and the light was better here than in my office in the back.

The poor little guy looked asleep, but nothing we'd done had managed to wake him.

Most of my championship purse had gone into making sure my sister could buy this place with as small a mortgage as possible. It was Amber's shop, but both Aunt Lizzie and I owned a share since we both put in most of the money she used to buy it.

After our mom disappeared, Aunt Lizzie took us in and raised us. Back in her day, she was probably the most famous showgirl in Vegas. When that day ended, she reinvented herself as a costume designer.

Vegas is all about acting like you're the biggest, best, and most important. Exquizite wasn't small potatoes, more midsized, but we got more than our share of contracts to provide the costuming for shows on the strip. Some of that was due to our collective contacts, but most of it had to do with Lizzie's skill and genius. Amber was very good but not quite at Aunt Lizzie's level yet.

"Pretty sure. Hootie here can move faster than a hummingbird and hover in place. You ever hear of an owl who could do that?" I asked. "Besides, he and Wayne are intelligent. I mean, people smart. They understand English."

"See, Rufus, there's hope that one day you will too," Amber said.

"Thanks, sis. What would I do without you?"

"Spend a lot more time stuck in trunks, I'd imagine," Amber said.

"And this Wayne is a... batsquatch?" Tiffany said.

"That's what I said. Why is this so difficult for you to believe?"

"Look, I don't even believe in regular sasquatches, let alone a blue one who flies around on bat wings. Maybe you're a little batty," Tiffany said.

"No more so than I was this morning."

"Which, in all fairness, is pretty batty," Amber said.

"It's nice to know I can always count on you, sis."

Amber gave me the big-sister look. "Like tonight, when I went to save your ass from a bunch of guys with guns? You mean like then?"

"Exactly like then."

"And you're saying a simple cheater tail job ended up with you at this Cryptid Fight Club where Bigfoot and the Loch Ness monster were throwing down?" Tiffany said.

"I didn't see either one, but there was a poster advertising a match between Bigfoot and a yeti last week."

"But that makes no sense. If someone had actually managed to catch mythical creatures, why make them fight each other in an underground club?" Tiffany asked. "You'd be instantly famous in scientific circles."

"And do people make a lot of money discovering new species in these scientific circles?" I asked.

"Probably not, but they can still put them on exhibit at one of the big hotels on the strip and charge people to come see them."

"And get all the animal rights activists protesting and demanding the cryptids be set free?" Amber said. "Seems like a fight club is the way to make the money, keep it a secret so the government doesn't take the cryptids away because I doubt the feds would reimburse them. And maybe the people who are able to catch creatures that most of the world thinks are imaginary have a good reason for not wanting to be in the spotlight themselves."

Sis had an interesting point. "Why would that be?"

Amber shrugged and shook her blonde hair out of her face.

"Beats me, but there are a lot of folks in Vegas happy getting big money and not being a household name. Like most of Aunt Lizzie's in-laws."

The Baronuto family doesn't like to be talked about, so we try to honor their wishes. Safer all around that way.

Tiffany got a rather worried look on her face as she ran her fingers through her long black hair. "You don't think that…"

"I don't. And neither do you," I said.

"If you didn't see the boss, then how do you know?"

"I didn't recognize anybody." I've done my best to avoid any professional dealings with Aunt Lizzie's in-laws. However, the Baronutos are a very close family, and when Aunt Lizzie took us in, that meant we were invited to a lot of family parties. If they were involved, I would've recognized somebody, and they would've recognized me.

And my first call would've been to Aunt Lizzie, not Amber.

"Do either of you have any ideas on how to help Hootie?"

"He hasn't touched the water or the peanut butter," Amber said.

"Did you ever consider that this dingbat might not eat peanut butter?" Tiffany said.

"Don't be ridiculous. All animals eat peanut butter." As if to accentuate her point, my sister plunged her spoon in and scooped out a huge gob. Tiffany shook her head, so Amber held up the spoon. "You want some?"

Tiffany made a face then turned back to me. "Sorry, Rufus. None of us had any pets growing up, let alone an owl. I got nothing. Maybe you should take him to a vet."

I sighed but nodded as Tiffany typed on her phone. "Here's one that opens soon and claims to specialize in exotic animals."

That would be a big selling point in Vegas. We probably have more lions, tigers, and enormous snakes per capita than any other place in the world.

"How will I explain the antlers?" I said.

"You'll think of something," Amber said.

CHAPTER TWELVE

Tiffany made a couple of calls, and it turns out the animal trainer at the show we did security for used the exotic animal vet. I called, making sure to name drop, and she agreed to come in early at six-thirty to take care of Hootie. I just said I had a hurt bird. She didn't ask any questions once I said I'd pay a ridiculous emergency fee.

I put Hootie in a cardboard box with some shredded paper on the bottom. He'd already made a mess on Aunt Lizzie's workbench, which freaked all three of us out. Aunt Lizzie is beyond OCD about her work area. We scrubbed it down better than any murderer had ever cleaned up a crime scene, but we knew we weren't likely to sneak it by her. Aunt Lizzie had the uncanny ability to tell if anything was different about her personal space. Tiffany took the better part of valor and left to get some sleep. Amber offered to go to the vet in my place as Aunt Lizzie usually showed up for work around eight.

I declined and got to the vet's office early. It was a simple white building with a sign out front that read *Wild Thingz Veterinary Clinic: Exotic animals a specialty*. The Z as an S was big in Vegas.

The light was on, so I took my box o' dingbat and went inside. An electronic chime announced my entrance.

"I'll be with you in a moment. Getting everything set for you back here," came a woman's voice.

"No problem." I wore a new set of recording glasses and took them off to check that they were on. I bought six at a time. They were cheaper that way. I was down to three. "I appreciate you fitting me into your schedule."

"Happy to do it, although I will admit to being a little tired. My night was crazy."

"An emergency call?" I asked.

"Something like that. I'm all ready for you. Why don't you come on back?"

As soon as I saw the vet's face, I recognized her, but it took me a couple of seconds to realize from where. She was the woman who had run into the fight cage to tend to the injured giant sloth that lost the match.

My first reaction was to leave as quickly as I could. I had developed an alias that I used whenever making appointments with someone I didn't know. It wasn't so much a false identity as someone who had his own address, private mailbox, and credit history. I based the last name on my MMA hero, the Iceman. I could fake an emergency phone call and leave, and she'd have no idea who I really was.

But me turning tail wasn't going to do anything to help Hootie. Like it or not, the woman who tended to the cryptids after the fights was probably the most qualified person to take care of the dingbat.

"Hello, Mr. Liddell, I'm Dr. Loraine Cliff," she said, motioning me into an examination room. "You said you found a hurt wild bird that you couldn't identify? After we get the little fella or gal patched up, I can give you the phone number for a nearby wildlife sanctuary that would be willing to take the bird in."

"Do they specialize in cryptids like you do?"

I smiled as her face froze. Not everybody who lives in Vegas is a good actor.

The vet had trouble getting words out. "I specialize in exotic animals. What's a cryptid?"

"There's Bigfoot, of course. Nessie too. But there's also Mantis Men from New Jersey and big old sloths from the Amazon. You know, that patient you were taking care of during your crazy night after the people you work for had two rare animals fight and tear the crap out of each other for a paying audience."

The vet's hand trembled, and she had trouble meeting my eyes, although she did a pretty good job of staring at my forehead. "I'm afraid I don't know what you're talking about. You need to leave."

"I was at your little Cryptid Fight Club, Dr. Cliff. So was my friend." I put the box down on the treatment table and opened the top.

The vet covered her mouth, took a deep breath, then stepped away from me. "You're the one who stole the dingbat!"

"More like aided his escape. This little guy was trying to get out of the theater through the vents. Probably would've made it too if he didn't stop and drag me to get his friend," I said.

The vet's head tilted like a cocker spaniel listening to a dog whistle. "Wait... are you trying to tell me that this dingbat exhibited higher cognitive behavior and empathy for another being on a level akin to a human?"

"Yes. Weren't you listening?"

"Wait... *You're* the idiot who let the batsquatch out of his cage? Do you have any idea how dangerous that creature is? He could have killed you and dozens of the people who were at Spot 51."

"Yeah, and I could've dated the homecoming queen in high school. Doesn't mean either of those things would really happen. In fact, my blue friend, along with my feathered pal here, got away, but they came back to pull my fat out of the fire. Because of that, my blue buddy got recaptured."

"You're anthropomorphizing. The batsquatch is a primate with some similarities to humans, but he's nothing more than an animal. He's not your friend. He's a beast."

"I beg to differ. A beast wouldn't sacrifice his freedom for mine. And this little guy flew in front of me and took the full brunt of one of those giant electric prods. He's breathing, but he won't wake up. You're going to fix him."

The vet laughed in my face with the arrogance of a producer on the strip. "You're in no position to tell me what to do. Right now, there are some very bad people scouring the city to find you. One phone call from me, and your life is over."

"Yours wouldn't be too pretty either if you did that. I'm recording this conversation. You just admitted to being part of a conspiracy to murder me and taking part in an illegal fight club. Unlike me, you'll be alive but facing criminal charges if I turn up dead since my associates will have this recording." My phone was sticking out of my shirt pocket. She stared at it, incorrectly assuming that that was how I was recording. "And you'll need more than just a criminal defense attorney since the state of Nevada will have no choice but to take your veterinary license away for being part of unethical and illegal brutality toward animals. Go ahead, make that call and I'll hit send. Maybe your murdering friends will get me. Perhaps I'll get them. If I survive, I think it'd be fun to testify before a state licensing board.

I got some nice shots of the fight and you running out to help the poor, sliced-up sloth."

"You mean the Mapinguari?" She grinned like she had won a prize. "Your recording will show me helping it."

"It will show you waiting until after it was hurt by a giant mantis in a fight for the enjoyment of paying spectators before you bothered to try." That knocked the smile off her face. "Look, instead of mutually assured destruction, why don't you take a look at this little guy and see what you can do to help him?"

When you ask a question like that, it's not unreasonable to expect a yes or no answer. Instead, the vet turned on the waterworks. You might think me a little cold, but a woman crying is the quickest way to make sure that I will not believe a word that follows.

That didn't mean I couldn't play along. I gently patted her on the shoulder, taking extra care to make the movements seem awkward.

"Why are you crying, Doc?"

Maybe my earlier assessment of her acting ability had been premature. As she looked up, the waterworks slowed as if on cue. The double sniff, followed by wiping her tears away with the back of her hand was a nice flourish.

"You think I want to be there to watch those magnificent animals rip each other to shreds? I'm a veterinarian. I've dedicated my life to healing animals, not helping them get hurt."

"I think that maybe the ones you helped put to sleep might disagree. Put any cryptids to sleep, Doc?"

"No!" she shouted with what seemed like genuine indignity. "Mr. Cabeza would take it out on me if anything happened to any of those animals. It's my job to patch them up and keep them alive. They can't make any money off a dead cryptid."

"How did they get so many cryptids in the first place?"

"Mr. Cabeza is some sort of hunter savant. He finds and catches them. I..." She paused as if trying to force herself from weeping openly. "...have no choice but to do what he says."

"Assuming I believe you, what made you sign up then?"

"Gambling debts. I'm not very good at picking who wins European football games."

"You live in Vegas, the international home of legal gambling, including betting on soccer. How could you possibly get in debt to a criminal?"

"You mean besides a case of incredible stupidity? My contract here at the clinic specifically forbids any employee from participating in gambling of any type. The owner had an issue with a former veterinarian who pawned a bunch of the clinic's equipment to cover his debts to a casino. The contract clause is his attempt to stop that from happening again. But you're right. The casinos don't charge interest. I won't pay off the vig if I live to be a hundred. Mr. Cabeza offered me a deal. Work at Spot 51 patching up all the injured cryptids for five years, and he wipes my debt clean."

"Five years seems like a long time to sign on for considering what a vet gets paid normally."

Her cheeks reddened with what seemed like genuine embarrassment. "Originally, it was two years, but Mr. Cabeza didn't cut me off. I had a serious losing streak during the last world cup, which upped my time to five years." The tears started flowing again, and she grabbed onto my arm for dear life. "You have to believe me."

This is America. I didn't have to believe anything. Or I could believe in stuff that was obviously untrue nonsense. "You helping my feathered friend here would go a long way toward me believing what you're saying."

"Absolutely." She put her hand on the door. "Let me go get..."

I pushed the door closed. "A moment ago, you threatened to make a phone call that would end my life. I'm not letting you out of my sight."

"Of course." The vet smiled, but her eyes glared daggers. She opened up some fancy cabinets. In short order, she had an IV bag hung, then moved aside a bunch of feathers to put a needle in the top of Hootie's leg. I was surprised at how long his legs were. With all the feathers, he seemed only to have ankles and talons.

"This dingbat is one of the most resilient cryptids I've ever seen. No injury seems to keep him down for long."

"Then why is he not waking up?"

"He received a tremendous shock to his system."

"Ha, ha. You're hilarious, Doc."

"I wasn't making a joke. You've seen the way he flies around. It uses up a tremendous amount of calories. He simply doesn't have enough energy left to do anything more than sleep. I'm giving him fluids with high amounts of glucose."

She placed a stethoscope to Hootie's ribs but didn't seem overly distraught by anything she heard. Next, she parted his chest feathers to reveal a burn where the prod zapped him, then rubbed ointment onto the seared skin. The matching burn on my back could have used some.

From the sounds outside, other people had come into the office, but Dr. Cliff stayed put and silent.

She seemed antsy and chewed on her bottom lip. "This could take a while. You can leave him with me and come back later."

"So you can score points by giving Mr. Cabeza back his missing dingbat? And set up an ambush for me? Nope."

"I have other patients to see, and this could take all day."

As if to prove her wrong, Hootie opened his eyes, flapped his wings, and landed on my shoulder, wrapping his wings around my neck in a hug.

"You're okay!"

The dingbat nodded, his antlers moving close enough to my eye that it made me nervous, but they didn't touch me.

"See—as good as new. Let me take out that needle."

Hootie hadn't noticed Cliff until she spoke. The dingbat crawled around to the back of my neck to get away from her. He bent over and pulled out the needle with his beak, flinging it away with a flick of his neck. The white bird flew across the room to pluck the metal top off a glass canister of dog biscuits then proceeded to devour them.

"As I said, he needs a lot of calories to function."

"What does he eat? Besides dog biscuits."

"Pretty much anything, including some things that would be poisonous to humans, but his favorite is peanut butter."

Amber was going to love hearing that almost as much as Tiffany would hate it.

"I did as you asked. I have other clients to see, so if you'll kindly leave, that would be great."

"Wait. Let's say I believe your story." Maybe I did. Just a little. "You can't enjoy watching those cryptids be beaten and torn apart every night. Why don't you help me get them out?"

"Besides the threat of a slow and painful death? I don't know where Spot 51 keeps the animals between fights. The club usually stays a week per location, but thanks to your antics last night, they relocated early. I don't even know where tonight's match is. They'll pick me up a couple of hours before."

"According to the posters I saw, the batsquatch has another fight tonight. I could follow when they pick you up, and you could help me sneak in to break the batsquatch out. If we show him to the authorities, it would lend a lot of weight to our story, and the cops could shut this down. If they can get enough to convict Mr. Cabeza, your debt goes away."

Which may or may not be true, depending on if he has a direct successor who can lay claim to his debts. But hey, this lady participated willingly. Wayne didn't.

"They're meticulous and allow just one route in and out. I'm sure security is on high alert now. The only way you're getting inside is with a ticket. And since they'll recognize you, I doubt that's going to work."

Maybe I could work around that.

"If I manage to get inside, where would the batsquatch be? And would you help me free him?"

"Typically, they keep the cryptids who'll be fighting separate and away from the main room."

Which lined up with Wayne's cage being in a back dressing room.

"They always have three matches per fight card?"

"Sometimes, there's only two. Depends on the popularity of the fighters."

"And where do they put you?"

"I usually get a tent behind the ring, so they don't have far to move any injured cryptids, and I can work on them out of the view of the paying customers."

"So, if I get in and find you, would you at least tell me where to find him?"

The vet glared at me, her jaw muscles tightening. Pissed, her arms cleared off a counter, and she kicked a garbage can.

"Do you have any concept of how dangerous that would be? What might happen to me?"

"Yes. But if you're serious about not wanting to be there and want to set things right, do you see any other way of making that happen?"

The vet stood there, her hands fisted so tightly that her knuckles were white. She chewed on her lower lip like it was a piece of gum. Hootie moved onto my shoulder and stared right at her. She couldn't seem to look directly at him.

After a grunt that sounded like she was passing a kidney stone, she said, "Fine. I'll help, but if you get caught, you've never heard of me."

"Fair enough. But just to be clear, if you double-cross me, I'll tell them you hired me to take the animals in the first place."

Our eyes locked on each other like rusty bear traps, but when we looked away, we had an understanding.

Chapter Thirteen

Some clients prefer to meet at my office while others want me to come to them. The latter was the case with Betty Lareau. Her house was in Summerlin North, a rather exclusive part of Vegas. I couldn't afford to rent a doghouse in her neighborhood.

After dropping Hootie off with Amber and watching him devour two jars of peanut butter, I'd called to let Mrs. Lareau with my good news. She wanted me to tell her over the phone, but my policy is to report everything in person. Even though it was only late morning, Mrs. Lareau answered the door wearing a slinky red dress far more appropriate for a night clubbing than sitting around the house.

Mrs. Lareau was at least a decade older than her husband's mistress and lacked her surgically enhanced measurements. Nevertheless, she was a beautiful woman, and the satin dress she wore showed off her natural curves to her full advantage. It was thin enough to leave little doubt that other than her four-inch stiletto heels, the dress was the only item of clothing she wore. Other than age and cup size, the mistress didn't have anything on the wife. In fact, Betty Lareau was far prettier.

Growing up around half-naked showgirls, I was taught better manners than to stare anywhere but at a woman's face. Judging by her expression, I disappointed her.

I typically greet clients with a handshake. Mrs. Lareau ignored my extended arm and instead enveloped me in a hug. Given that Mrs. Lareau was about five foot nine before she put on the four-inch heels, it made the placement of my head awkward. My client didn't seem to mind. In fact, she shifted position twice, so my face rested in her cleavage.

She pulled away slowly while running her hands down my arms, stopping to give my biceps a gentle squeeze.

"You're a lot more solid than you look. Do you work out?"

Even though I knew it was a line to stroke my male ego, I still found myself pleased. I was professional enough, however, to steer the conversation back to business. "I didn't come here to discuss my workout routine, Mrs. Lareau."

She giggled and touched my shoulder. "Please call me Betty. Being called Mrs. makes me feel so old. I don't look old to you, do I, Rufus?"

"No, Betty, you do not."

The answer made her smile. "How old do you think I am, Rufus?"

I knew her age from my background check, but I was no dummy. Never guess someone's weight and always subtract a few years off their age. "Twenty-six, maybe twenty-seven?"

That made her beam. "Thirty-six last month." Betty took me by the hand. "Come… tell me about all the nasty things you caught my soon-to-be ex-husband doing." She led me to a den and motioned me to sit in what was either a tiny loveseat or a very large chair.

"Can I get you a drink, Rufus?"

"No, thank you."

Smiling, she squeezed in next to me. She didn't have to sit so close. There were a few unoccupied inches of room on the other side of the seat, not to mention three other chairs. I would have slid away, but she hadn't left me any room, and honestly, her nearness felt good.

"Your suspicions were correct. Mr. Lareau is indeed cheating on you."

Gritted teeth replaced her smile. Betty didn't seem to trust herself to speak, so I continued.

"I followed him for three days. Each day he met with this woman." I held up a tablet displaying a picture of the blonde.

Betty found her voice. "Henry chose that plastic slut over me? Her boobs are so big they don't even look real. What is she? A stripper?"

I shook my head. "A cocktail waitress." That's nothing to sneeze at in Vegas. "Her name is Tammy Hayes."

"I'd like to scratch the little bitch's eyes out."

"Betty, I recommend you have no contact with her. I'm not a lawyer, but you will look less sympathetic in front of any judge if you go after her in any way. Not to mention you'd open yourself up to civil liability. Why give her any of the money you'll get in the divorce?"

Betty nodded then smoothed out her red dress. "You're right, of course. Do you have proof he's screwing her?"

I nodded. "Are you sure you want to see this?"

Betty involuntarily gulped a lungful of air and forgot to let it out. When she realized, she exhaled it all at once like she was halfheartedly blowing out birthday candles. "I *need* to see it."

As much as some people think they want or need to see proof that the spouse is cheating when the moment comes, it can be quite traumatizing. To minimize that, I had brought stills instead of showing her the videos.

I started with pictures of him picking her up and taking her into the motel room. Him picking Tammy up in the Lamborghini and her head disappearing into his lap.

Betty ground her teeth, and her nails dug into the cushion we sat on.

The slideshow moved on to hubby making out and groping his side dish at Spot 51, including a zoomed-in shot of him reaching under her dress. Next was the walk to the men's room and shots of them in the stall, which were quite graphic and left no doubt that Mr. Lareau had sex with a woman who was not his wife.

"That bastard! How could he do this to me after nine years of marriage?"

I stayed quiet. It wasn't the type of question she really wanted answered.

"Is there video or just pictures?"

"I have video that I'd be happy to send directly to your divorce lawyer," I said, wanting to spare her from watching.

"I need to see it."

"Are you sure? Watching him with her will burn itself into your memory and stay with you forever."

"I want it to stay with me forever. I need it to motivate me to take this clown for everything he has. I was loyal our entire marriage. Not a week went by where some guy didn't hit on me or make me an offer. Hell, every one of his scumbag friends propositioned me at some point, but I turned them all down, even the hot one, because I loved that idiot, and I believed in the sanctity of our marriage. As far as I'm concerned, right now, we are divorced. The rest is just paperwork. I hate that a part of me still loves him. If that part doesn't see absolute proof, it will feel sorry for him and stop me from punishing him for breaking our marriage vows. Do you understand?"

I nodded. Calling up the video, I handed her the tablet.

She pressed the sideways triangle, and the video played, complete with sound.

Holding the tablet, she stood and circled the room. The more she watched, the faster her pace became. When it was over, she screamed and tossed my tablet into a wall, shattering it.

That happens a lot, which is why I also buy cheap tablets in bulk.

Realizing what she did, she looked at me and cringed. "I'm so sorry about that."

"Forgivable under the circumstances, although I will have to add that to my expense report." I took the tri-folded piece of paper out of my suit jacket pocket along with a pen, added the retail price of the tablet, and handed the invoice to Betty. "This is my bill. A soon as payment is made, I'll send you the sign-in information for the FTP site with all the pictures and video."

Betty looked at the bill and pointed to one line. "What's this charge for three thousand dollars for damaged recording devices?"

"I was wearing two recording devices following your husband. They were broken in a scuffle with club security."

"Why not just use a phone?"

"Because people get suspicious when you point a phone in their direction. And the club he went to makes people check their cell phones." They still had mine, in fact. I tried to track it using an app, but that was a bust. They must've destroyed it. I included it on the bill under miscellaneous. "I know it seems pricey, but I can provide an invoice to prove that's how much they're worth."

"No, that's fine. It's a small price to pay for proof that will get me millions. In fact, I'll pay this right now." She picked her cell phone off a table. Using the routing numbers on my bill, she transferred the funds.

My phone buzzed, letting me know I got paid. I checked to make sure the amount was right. It wasn't.

It was twenty-five grand higher than it should have been.

"I think you may have transferred too much."

Betty smiled and shook her head. "I transferred the right amount of money. You came through for me, Rufus, when nobody else did. I think you deserve a bonus."

"Twenty-five thousand is an exceptionally generous bonus. Thank you."

Betty strutted back to the cozy seat and stood a few feet in front of me, then giggled again.

"That's not your bonus, silly. It was a tip."

I sat mesmerized as something red slid to the floor.

"This is your bonus."

"I'm sorry, but you're a client, and I can't..."

"I paid you, and our business is concluded, which means I'm no longer your client."

I couldn't argue with her logic. It was the most enjoyable bonus ever.

Sometime later, with Betty's blessing, I sat on her porch and waited for her soon-to-be ex-husband to come home. While I was waiting, a locksmith showed up and changed all the locks. It turns out Betty was really going to clean up in the divorce proceedings. Henry Lareau had put the condo and several other assets, including the Lamborghini, in her name for tax reasons I'd never have to worry about.

To rescue Wayne, I needed to figure out the new location of Cryptid Fight Club and how to get in. Since the vet was no help, I had to try another way. Logic, with a large dose of hope, led me to the conclusion that if Henry Lareau had tickets to one night of CFC, he might have tickets to another.

The fight poster dated for tonight listed a match between the batsquatch and something called a cherufe. According to Google, that was a reptilian humanoid that supposedly lives in volcanoes. Oddly enough, so did the batsquatch. Unlike my hairy blue friend with the wings, cherufe eat human flesh. According to one website, they can also spit globs of lava or fireballs. That didn't sound like something I'd like to be in a fight cage with.

I texted Amber to check on Hootie. The dingbat was fine, but Amber was out of peanut butter, jelly, bread, and chocolate. So far, he was doing a good job hiding from both customers and Aunt Lizzie.

When the green Lamborghini finally pulled in, I reached behind my shoulder and rang the doorbell. Betty had requested that so she could watch on her doorbell cam.

Henry Lareau stomped up the walk, glaring at me the whole way.

"Who the hell are you, and what are you doing on my porch?"

I stood up slowly, and when he got to the bottom of the steps, recognition glinted in his eyes.

"You're that pipsqueak from last night. The one that kidnapped the dingbat and tried to steal the batsquatch."

"Rescue," I corrected.

"What are you? One of those animal-rights kooks? You stole, pure and simple. I'm sure the cops would agree. The fact that you stalked me back to my home is something else I think the cops would be interested in." He pulled out his cell. "How about I just give them a call?"

I shrugged. "Go ahead, Hank, get them down here."

"Don't call me Hank," he growled.

"Sure thing, Hank. While I'm getting right on that, you make that call. I'm sure the people behind Cryptid Fight Club would love to hear about how you blabbed all about their setup to the police."

Lareau glared at me but lowered his phone.

"What are you doing at my house, pipsqueak?"

I bit my tongue instead of pointing out to him that the house was in his soon-to-be ex-wife's name. He'd find that out soon enough with no help from me.

"I had some other business in the neighborhood, so I decided to wait and chat with you regarding Spot 51. I want your tickets to tonight's Cryptid Fight Club match along with the address of where it's going to take place."

"And I want to be a billionaire. I guess neither of us will be getting what we want."

"Wrong. I'm not leaving until I get those tickets."

Lareau acted like a tough guy and rolled up his sleeves, then lifted his fists, pretending he knew how to use them. "Then I guess I'm going to have to make you leave."

Hank looked rather disappointed when his tough-guy act didn't scare me, then seemed confused when I rolled my eyes.

"Hank, let's save you a beating and a lot of hospital bills, shall we? My name is Rufus Griffin. Take your phone and Google me. I'll wait."

Lareau had no idea why I wasn't making any attempt to leave or attack him, but he began typing with his index finger.

His thumb hit search, and I watched his pupils go wide.

I couldn't help but grin. No matter how much I paid for search engine optimization, the first item a search showed about me was always my title bout, not my PI business.

Lareau did a triple take, looking back and forth from the phone to me.

"That's me. Go ahead and watch the first video. I'm in no rush."

Lareau eventually turned off his phone and looked up at me.

He wore a fake smile, and his fists were gone.

"Perhaps I was hasty with my earlier words. I guess we can talk, but I gotta tell you there's a camera in the doorbell, so if you touch me, I'll sue your ass and see you in jail. And I'm not telling or giving you anything."

"If that's how you want to play it, sure. I know someone who would be very interested that you're having sex with Tammy Hayes."

His meekness vanished as he jabbed his finger toward my face. "You better not tell my wife. Besides, you have no proof."

I flipped my phone over to reveal a picture of him groping Tammy at Spot 51. "Want to bet?"

He smiled. "You don't know what you're talking about. That woman's my wife."

"Really? Let's knock on the door so you can introduce me to her."

Beads of sweat formed on Lareau's forehead. "She's not home right now. She's at work."

"Nice try, Hank. Tammy's not your wife. Your wife is a lot prettier."

"Fine. How about I give you five hundred bucks to walk away and not show that picture to anybody?"

I shook my head. "Doesn't really work for me, Hank. I find it amusing that you're cheating on your wife with Tammy while she's cheating on her boyfriend with you. Weird, right?"

Henry froze, and his skin looked like all the blood drained away from his body.

"You know who Tammy's boyfriend is, right?" I didn't need to wait for an answer. His sudden pallor told me he knew. "Samm Wyde, two-time SFF heavyweight champion. Samm is a big boy. Me, I'm just a welterweight. Samm is on hiatus right now, going for counseling to control his anger issues. I can't imagine what he'll think of this picture. I don't think the threat of a doorbell camera would stop him from him beating you into primordial ooze."

I raised my phone and dramatically held my index finger over the screen.

"In exactly sixty seconds, I'm going to hit send on this text to Samm with this picture and your name. The only things that will stop this from happening are your CFC tickets and the location of tonight's match. The timer starts now."

"You wouldn't!"

I grinned and wiggled my eyebrows.

"I'll give you a grand not to."

"Fifty-two seconds left, Hank, and sadly for you, I don't see any tickets."

Henry sprinted back to the Lamborghini, opened the driver's side scissor door, and dove across the seats to open the glove compartment.

"Thirty-nine seconds, Hank."

He got out of the car and walked far too slowly toward me.

"Twenty-six seconds, Hank. Twenty-five..."

Henry sprinted up the walk and held out a second cell phone.

I took it. "Eighteen seconds and the phone isn't unlocked, and I don't have an address."

Lareau grabbed the phone and held it up to his eye. The retina scan unlocked it.

"Yes, you do. The ticket barcode is in the Spot 51 app. Fifty-one minutes before the doors open, the app will give you driving directions via GPS."

I hit the app button. "What's the password?"

Lareau looked sheepish and whispered, "Boobs2. First b is capitalized."

I entered it, and the app opened. The tickets were there with a counter ticking down the time until the doors opened.

"You made it with less than a second to spare." I opened the phone settings to change the password and shut off the retina scan.

"So, you won't send the photo?"

I held the phone up to his eye to scan it, so the phone let me change the password. He didn't complain.

"I won't send that photo so long as the folks behind CFC have no idea that I'm coming. If they do, I will be instructing my colleagues to send it, along with a video of you and Tammy in the men's room stall, to Samm if anything happens to me. And there is no expiration on that. Ever." Yeah, if something ever does happen to me, a lot of people of going to be very upset that their secrets are sent to the person they least want to know them.

"They won't hear it from me. And you won't mention anything to my wife?"

"Don't have to. She's already seen them."

"What!?"

The doorbell screeched with static. "That's right, you son of a bitch. I know everything about you and your plastic tramp!"

Lareau pushed past me and tried to get his key in the door. It didn't fit. I waved as I walked away to the screams of Betty kicking him out. As I passed the Lamborghini, I noticed that the key fob sat on the seat and watched as the open driver door scissored down to close and lock.

Betty must have used the spare set to lock it up from inside the house.

Looks like old Hank was not only homeless, but he'd be walking.

Chapter Fourteen

"This plan has got to be the stupidest idea you've ever come up with," Amber said none too quietly.

It wasn't. That distinction belonged to a case where I had to get three kids out of an abusive house back when I worked for CPS. I could've lost my job and gone to jail. This was more dangerous because if it didn't work, I was a dead man.

Putting myself in danger to help others may be a character flaw, but it was also a huge part of who I am.

It's not something I like to talk about, but when I was eleven years old, I was kidnapped by a psycho. I got out alive. Not all his other victims were so lucky, and the list of kids he'd hurt went back years. I was pretty messed up afterward, and Amber would be the first to point out that I still was. It's a big reason I went to work for Child Protective Services. I wasn't going to let what happened to me happen to anybody else because, believe it or not, that type of horror show is usually run by a member of the victim's family. In my case, the guy was pretty much a stranger.

I left gainful employment at CPS when the rules became more important than those we were supposed to be protecting.

"I agree with your sister, Rufus," Tiffany said. Hootie buzzed up and hovered in front of her face, shaking his feathered head. "Listen, bird, the odds of Rufus pulling this off are astronomical. The smart move is to let the cops handle it."

"These guys have been running this operation for a long time. That means somewhere along the line, they found a way to either outsmart law enforcement or get them on the payroll. I've got no way of figuring out which." Most cops are decent, but the few that aren't do a lot to destroy the reputation of all police. "I ask their cop on the inside for help, *and* poof, quicker than the best magic show on the strip, they make me disappear."

As Amber listened, she also scooped balls of peanut butter out of a jar with a spoon, flinging them up in the air. Aunt Lizzie had gone home, but we were in my office in case she came back. Normally, I'd be upset if someone was throwing peanut butter around my place of business, but Hootie caught them in his beak and devoured them in about a blink and a half. The dingbat's speed was impressive, as was the fact that he was on his third jar of the new supplies Tiff had picked up. He preferred crunchy. By my rough estimate, so far, he'd already eaten about three-quarters of his body weight in peanut butter.

"It's not worth dying for some animal," Tiffany said.

"That animal saved my life."

"Then wouldn't you be doing him a disservice by throwing it away?" Tiffany said.

"That's not how it works."

"It is for most people. Why risk probable death for this batsquatch?"

I spoke so low my voice was practically a whisper. "You know why. He's helpless and alone, trapped by people who mean him harm. If I don't go, there ain't nobody coming to save him. I can't allow that to happen to someone else if I can help it. And I can help Wayne."

Tiffany kissed my cheek and messed my hair. "You are so broken."

She wasn't wrong. This situation pushed all my buttons and twirled my dials up to eleven. When I thought about what was happening to Wayne, all my mind saw was me in that dark, stone basement, with no light and a dirt floor, chained to a wall, never knowing if I was going to last another day or if I would ever see sunlight or my family again.

I don't want to go into what I had to eat to survive, but let's just say they were crunchy and had lots of legs.

Nobody came for me then, but last night a batsquatch came back for me. If I didn't do the same for him, I'd never be able to live with myself.

"You know you're not going to talk Rufus out of it. If I thought it would help, I'd try myself," Amber said. "We need to do whatever we can to make sure he gets out alive."

"Which is why you should be taking me in as your plus one," Tiffany said.

I shook my head. What I wanted to say was that it was too danger-ous, but that would just push all of her buttons, so instead, I went with,

"I'm going to have a hard enough time trying to pass myself off as Lareau. You'll never pass for Tammy." Tiffany opened her mouth, and I cut her off. "You look nothing like her."

"You look nothing like Lareau."

"I will by the time Amber's done with me. Besides, the gatekeepers are men. They are much more likely to pay attention to how a woman looks than a man. I can alter my appearance. In a skimpy dress, you won't be able to fake her proportions. Or her skin tone." Tiff was black, Tammy white. Plus, Tiffany was a whole lot prettier, but I wasn't about to say that. Our relationship is too complicated for casual compliments.

"You have a point, but you've also got not one, but two people who could open their mouths and sell you down the river."

"If that happens, it'll be up to you guys to follow through on my threats to each of them."

"What about the bird?"

"Hootie stays here with Amber."

The dingbat heard and hovered in front of my face, hooting in a very argumentative tone.

"Hootie, I'm sorry. I know Wayne is your friend too, but if something happens to me, you'll be safe."

There was more angry hooting, and the bird flew over in the corner then turned away from me in an apparent pout.

"Now, let's figure out how to make this work."

I'm not brave or selfless. Pulling this kind of stunt is a character flaw, or so my shrink used to tell me.

Plus, I was terrified. I stopped the car twice with the intent of turning around and forgetting about the entire plan. Then I drove past the warehouse the GPS on the Spot 51 app told me to go to. I stopped the third time three miles down the road and texted Tiffany the warehouse location, which was several minutes outside of the town of Blue Diamond.

I would've done it a little closer to my destination, but there was no service near the place. I texted Tiffany that too. It also meant that I wouldn't be able to upload anything from my surveillance glasses, even if I could have worn them. Lareau didn't wear glasses, so it wouldn't make any sense for him to suddenly start. I had a tie-tack camera. It was more expensive than the recording glasses because it was so small and also had less memory and a lower quality picture. I'd be lucky to get an hour's worth of footage. Not that more would have mattered. If I was still in there after an hour, I probably wasn't coming out.

It was awful. I was driving a Lamborghini, and I couldn't even enjoy it.

Don't think that I had a Lamborghini stashed somewhere. Several services in Vegas rented high-end cars and had the same model in Verde Mantis, which is a rich-people way of saying green. It didn't hurt that it was also the most popular color in Vegas.

I hoped to have it back in twelve hours to save money, but both the timeframe and the bringing it back part may have been a bit too optimistic.

It might seem a tad too extravagant an expense, but I was impersonating Lareau. It wouldn't do to take the time to put on gel body padding, a wig, and even wear makeup just to be pegged as an imposter because I showed up in a five-year-old sedan.

It made me wish I had a paying client to charge the expense to.

I parked near the front, diagonally taking up two spaces. It was a jerk move, but it's exactly what Lareau always did.

I took a deep breath and did some mind-calming techniques that I used before a match. Back then, the goals were to win and to walk out under my own power. Who knew the option of being carried out on a stretcher would one day become so appealing?

I hid my latest burner phone under the seat. I brought Lareau's phone in.

As I stepped out of the car and closed the door, something grabbed my leg. I looked down and saw a familiar feathered friend wrapped around my ankle. He'd ignored me telling him to stay put—which truthfully, I admired—and somehow followed a Lamborghini to the desert twenty miles outside of Vegas. . Just because I wasn't exactly enjoying the Lamborghini didn't mean I didn't open it up. At one point, I hit 110 mph, yet the dingbat was able to keep up with me. That's nothing if not impressive.

I bent to tie my shoes. "Hootie, what are you doing here?"

The dingbat pointed his beak at me and then at the warehouse.

I didn't argue with a person—yes, I know Hootie was an animal, but he was intelligent, brave, and loyal, so I was granting him official personhood— this determined. It'd be pointless.

"I can't get you in hidden under my pant leg. They frisk people going in for guns. I'm not sure how to smuggle you inside, and if I waste too much time out here, security might get suspicious."

Hootie waved dismissively, then placed his wing on his chest before pointing at the warehouse.

"So, you'll get yourself in?" The antlered bird nodded. "And out, if necessary?"

The dingbat twisted its wing like it was someone's palm going up and down. The dingbat wasn't quite as confident about his exit.

"Stay hidden. You heard the plan back at Exquizite, so don't get involved unless you have to, understood?"

Hootie nodded, and I stood up. When I looked down again, the dingbat was gone.

I did my best to imitate Lareau's strut as I went to the front door. I unlocked his phone before I got there since I'd changed it to password mode. I had no way of knowing if security knew he used retina recognition.

It was a struggle not to stop short when I saw Cueball on door duty again. Amber had made me up so my face looked just like Henry Lareau's. Her makeup skills rivaled those people you see on YouTube transforming themselves into Johnny Depp or a Disney princess. This was going to be a real test of her work.

"Good evening, Mr. Lareau. Where's your lovely lady friend? Will she be joining us?" Cueball asked as he patted me down for weapons. I held my breath, hoping the gel padding wouldn't give me away. It felt like body fat, but would it fool a professional?

"The wife is starting to get suspicious, so I'm solo tonight."

The frisk ended, and Cueball gave me a conspiratorial smile. "Say no more, sir."

I held my phone up, and Cueball scanned the barcode on the screen. There were no alarms, just a ping. Cueball's smile never wavered as he checked my phone and handed me my claim ticket. "Enjoy CFC."

"I will."

As I walked through the metal detector, I was impressed that neither my hands nor my knees shook. I headed straight to the bar and ordered a cocktail. I had no intention of drinking it, but I've learned over years doing surveillance that people are less likely to look suspiciously at somebody wandering around a party with a drink in their hand.

Lareau had again sprung for table service, but I didn't go there. Instead, I wandered toward the fenced-in ring, which looked almost exactly like it had in the theater. Probably prefabricated, so it came apart and went back up quick and easy.

There was a tent behind, just like Dr. Cliff had told me. I pulled open the flap and barged in like I owned the place.

"This where I get my photo op with the cryptid fighters?" I asked, looking around the tent. Dr. Cliff was alone.

The intrusion had startled and annoyed the vet, who sat behind a card table serving as a makeshift desk. Cliff rose to her feet and came straight at me.

"Sir, this area is for authorized personnel only. You have to leave." The vet motioned me back toward the flap.

"Nonsense. I was promised a chance to take a selfie with the batsquatch, so where do I go to get it?"

With amusement, I watched her pupils expand, and her eyebrows rise.

"It's you, isn't it?" she whispered. I put my index finger over my lips.

"Just tell me where to go for that selfie, and I'll be out of your hair."

"The back of the warehouse wasn't entirely cleared out, and it's a maze. I can't give accurate directions." The vet looked down, took a deep breath, then lowered her chin until her gaze met mine. "I'll have to take you."

CHAPTER FIFTEEN

Security was surprisingly lax. Then again, I hadn't run into any in the back of the theater either, although I assumed that was because they were out chasing after Hootie. Maybe they just didn't bother guarding the cryptids. I mean, who's going to mess with a batsquatch or giant mantis willingly?

The vet was so nervous her lower lip trembled. She also had no clue about how to walk around like she belonged somewhere. She was bent forward at the waist and looking back and forth suspiciously as we tramped through a bunch of empty shelving units that did seem to have been pushed together as if somebody purposely made a maze. Maybe they had a minotaur back here.

"The batsquatch is in there." Dr. Cliff pointed to a door. I bent down and made like I was tying my shoes again when I was actually removing some items from hidden compartments in the built-up heel lifts of my shoes.

I stood and looked at the vet. "Thanks for coming through."

Cliff didn't say a word and seemed to nod as an afterthought.

This time the door wasn't even locked, so I opened it slowly. There was just the slightest bit of light, but it was enough for me to make out a cage with a familiar figure inside. I gently closed the door so nobody could sneak up behind me. The inside was crowded with more shelving units.

Wayne spotted me and began vocalizing and pointing all around the room.

"Wayne, it's okay. I'm here to get you out."

"Want to bet?"

My blood ran cold. I didn't need to turn around to know who had stepped out from behind the shelves to my right rear. The New York accent was too distinctive.

"You know, I've met a lot of losers in my time, but you are in a class by yourself. You got away clean. We had no idea who you were or how to find you, so what do you do? You walk right back into our operation. And for what? Some big, dumb, flying monkey. You know you'd never sell him without getting caught, right?"

The door creaked open and closed again.

"If Steve Liddell here—" The alias I used to make my vet appointment. "—is to be believed, he's not here for money but to do the right thing. He thinks the batsquatch is intelligent and saved his life," Dr. Cliff said from the back of the room.

"Well, he sort of did," Tall Drink said, stepping out from behind shelving to my back left.

I put my hands out to my sides and slowly turned around, unsurprised to see Brooklyn and Tall Drink pointing guns at me.

"Since the two of you seem to be passing out guns like party favors, how come you didn't give her one?" I glared at the vet, but she only smiled back.

"The doc doesn't need one. She's got us. And enough common sense to tell us about your idiot plan," Brooklyn said.

"I guess pointing out that you gave me your word wouldn't change a lot at this point?"

The vet laughed. "You think that coming to where I work and strong-arming me would get me to help you? Why wouldn't I screw you over?"

I smiled. "You didn't do this just to put the screws to me. How many years did betraying me take off your debt?"

The vet proudly puffed up her chest. "A year and a half."

"I bet Mr. Cabeza also doubled your credit limit as a thank you…" Her smile fell and smashed to bits as the truth sank in. "He could have taken away all five years and offered you credit and good odds, and by dinnertime, you'd be back in debt to him. You won't ever get free from these guys. And I can't think of anyone who deserves it more."

From her expression, I half expected a growl. Instead, she said, "It ain't like you're going to get away from them either, now is it?"

I shrugged. "That's yet to be determined."

Brooklyn and Tall Drink chuckled in two-part harmony.

"You've got nothing, and we've..."

Brooklyn was about to say that they had guns, but he should have just shut up. That's the thing in a street fight. Trash talk is lots of fun, but at some point, it needs to be ignored in favor of actually winning the fight.

And he was wrong about me not having anything.

I pressed the buttons on two lipstick-sized canisters hidden in the palms of my hands. Pepper stray flooded the gunmen's eyes, nostrils, and mouths, coming as a complete surprise, as did my fist in Tall Drink's face. With nobody but Wayne behind me, Tall Drink was closest. Taking a trick out of the Spot 51 goon playbook, I followed up with a homemade micro stun gun to the throat.

I grabbed the gun out of his hand before taking him the rest of the way down with a knee to the groin. I learned a long time ago, it's not fighting dirty when the other guys are trying to kill you.

I sent a flying forward kick toward Brooklyn's face. For those of you who haven't fought professionally, I'll point out that a flying kick to the face is normally a very stupid move. In this case, it was the fastest attack I could manage, and I gambled that Brooklyn wouldn't see it coming, thanks to the face full of pepper spray.

Landing on my feet, I smashed the barrel of Tall Drink's gun across Brooklyn's jaw. Grabbing hold of the wrist of his gun hand, I twisted Brooklyn's arm and smacked my gun barrel down on the spot on his elbow where the ulnar nerve isn't protected. Between that and the wrist twist, he dropped his gun, which I kicked away as I jabbed a fist and my gun barrel hard and fast into his throat. I moved behind him. Wrapping my arm around his neck, I squeezed. It didn't take long to choke him out and onto the floor.

With Brooklyn unconscious and Tall Drink curled up into a ball, I allowed myself to relax, which broke two of the cardinal rules of fighting. Don't underestimate someone, and don't stop until there's nobody left who can hurt you.

I quickly realized this mistake when I saw the traitorous veterinarian pick Brooklyn's gun and point it at my chest. I returned the favor with Tall Drink's gun.

"Put your hands over your head and drop the gun," Dr. Cliff ordered.

"I'm not going to do that, but that's stupid of you to ask. If I dropped the gun, there's a damn good chance it's going to go off when it hits the ground. I'd make sure to angle it toward you so, with a little luck, the bullet might hit you."

"Fine. Gently put the gun on the ground..."

"Save your breath and think this through. I just took these two guys out when they had guns, and I didn't. I'm willing to bet your life that you've never been in a situation anything like this. I get in fights for a living. You don't have a chance." Strictly speaking, that wasn't true. There are plenty of professional fighters who've gotten taken out by amateurs. A gun means all the strength and training in the world just went out a ten-story window backward after a hard night's drinking.

Didn't mean I wasn't going to try to convince her otherwise.

"You think we have a Mexican standoff? That we'll just point guns at each other, and if one of us shoots, both of us shoot? You forget to figure in your blue friend." The veterinarian pointed the gun away from me to focus instead on Wayne. "Drop your gun, or I shoot the batsquatch."

"Not going to happen." This is one situation I've played out in my head well over a hundred times. If I put down the gun, there's no way I don't lose.

"Then the batsquatch dies. You got five seconds, four..."

"If you shoot Wayne, Cabeza'll be pissed, and you'll die before Wayne does. If suicide is your game, fire away. It's obvious that you don't have any experience with a handgun. You're standing and holding it like someone in a movie. Sure, it looks cool, but it's not effective." Again, more mind games. It was true, but if she pulls the trigger, the gun will still work no matter how she stands or holds it. "Can you hit what you shoot at? It's not that easy the first hundred times. At a paper target, sure, not too hard. And Wayne's a big target, so you think you won't miss, but if this is your first shot ever, you probably will. So, to make sure it's harder, let's shrink the target. Wayne lay on the floor."

"You moron. It's a dumb animal..."

The evil vet shut up when Wayne did as I said.

"How?"

"I told you he's smart. I also figure he's seven feet tall and five hundred pounds."

"Closer to four thirty-five," the evil vet corrected.

"Which means he's got a body density equivalent to a bear. As a vet, what would you say the odds of a hunter going out with a handgun being successful in killing a bear?" I took steps backward, my aim never wavering from her chest. I made it to the side of the cage, where I plucked the keys off a shelf.

The evil vet's lower lip trembled.

"Not that good, right?" I sidestepped toward the cage and put the key in. "So, you could take that shot and just wound Wayne, which means you'd have died for nothing."

"But if you shoot me, you kill his best chance to be treated for the gunshot wound," the vet countered.

"Nope. Be too dangerous to let you try. After all, you'd just be trying to figure out another way to kill us."

I unlocked the door then pulled it open. "Come on out, buddy."

Wayne leapt like a jungle cat through the opening and landed on his feet, then reared up to his full height. I motioned for him to go to our left, and I moved to the right, using the same flanking maneuver that Brooklyn and Tall Drink tried.

"You can't shoot both of us. The moment you pull the trigger, no matter who it's pointed at, I shoot you. If you shoot me back, I'm pretty sure Wayne will take you out before you can aim at him. After all, you've seen him fight."

Which I hadn't, but I figured if he was a headliner, he had to be pretty impressive.

"What this all boils down to is that as long as that gun is in your hand, you are going to die. The only way for you to live is to gently place it on the floor and walk into that cage."

Dr. Cliff's eyes darted from the gun to the floor. "How do I know you won't kill me anyway?"

"You don't, but unlike you, my word means something. You do what I say with no funny business, and you'll be alive when I walk out of this room. Add this thought to your mental mix—I came back to risk my life for this blue furry fellow I just met yesterday. You think I'm going to kill you out of spite?"

The traitorous veterinarian lowered her gun to her side and stepped toward me like she was planning to hand it to me, but that wasn't what I'd told her to do. I charged her. Good thing, too, because she was already raising the gun barrel toward me when I smacked her on the side of her head with my weapon. It was a solid blow, and she crumpled to the ground.

Yeah, I know some people might be horrified at a man hitting a woman, but like I said before, there is no such thing as dirty fighting when the other person is trying to kill you.

I turned toward the batsquatch. "Are you okay?"

Wayne nodded, the blue fur on his head bobbing up and down like a heavy metal fan's hair in a mosh pit. He put his hands together and flapped them up and down like they were wings.

"Hootie is okay and around here somewhere. We need to get you out, and we're not risking the front door again. Help me get these three in your cage, and we'll see if there's a back way out."

The giant blue guy grinned as he tossed each of his unconscious captors across the room and into the cage using only one arm.

I picked up the other gun and tucked it in my waistband, making sure the safety was on. Slipping my homemade stun gun and one of the teeny tiny pepper sprays in a pocket, I turned toward the door, hoping there be no more surprises.

CHAPTER SIXTEEN

As we stepped into the warehouse proper, there was no one waiting for us.

"I came in from that way." I pointed to our left. "I think the back of the building is over there. Hopefully, there's a fire exit or window of some sort. Let's move as quickly and quietly as we can."

Before I knew what happened, a pair of strong blue hands picked me up, and the ground was suddenly very far away.

"Next time, give a guy some warning," I whispered as I traveled by batsquatch air over the shelving units toward the back wall of the warehouse.

Wayne touched down near a door that had been boarded up from the inside.

Putting my second gun in my waistband, I grabbed hold of one board, put a foot on the doorframe, and pulled. I felt the nails give ever so slightly. Unless I could find something to use as a crowbar, this was going to take a while.

Or maybe not. Wayne gently pushed me aside. He took hold of a board with each hand and pulled. They slid out of the wall like they'd been greased. He did the same for the last two boards when we heard a click and froze.

Someone pulled both guns out of my waistband and my wig off. Wayne tossed one board after the other, but the man behind me dodged both of them. Once he stopped moving, I realized it was Nibbles. He didn't look happy, even pointing his gun.

"Nice try, asshole, but now it's time for your little friend to die."

There was no pause between his last word and six shots as he emptied his revolver directly at my torso. I didn't feel a thing. Because none of the bullets hit me. Nibbles had to be the worst shot in history.

That's when I spotted Hootie hovering in front of me. I watched with fascination as he spit out six bullets.

Nibbles looked like he couldn't believe his eyes. Hell, I wasn't too sure about what I was seeing either. Using the automatic he pulled off me, the goon aimed a little higher this time and fired until he emptied the magazine. Hootie moved so fast he was a blur, but the dingbat somehow caught all ten bullets in his beak.

As shocked as he must have been, Nibbles still managed to toss aside the empty automatic, flip open his revolver's cylinder, and pull a speed loader out of his jacket pocket.

Grabbing one of the door planks off the floor, I smashed him in the face before he could close the cylinder. I was proud of myself. I made a conscious effort not to use the side with the nails. Although if he had managed to close the cylinder, I would have.

Blood spurted along his face from his crushed nose, but he didn't go down, only stumbled back. I swung the board at his right forearm, hoping he'd drop the gun. Unfortunately, not only did his forearm get smashed, but so were those gun-dropping hopes. He didn't let go. Nibbles was an honest-to-goodness tough guy.

Hootie must've figured out what I was trying to do because suddenly, he hovered by Nibbles' wrist and bit down hard on the space between his thumb and index finger. Nibbles grunted and loosened his grip, but the revolver still didn't fall. Turns out it didn't need to.

The slight weakening of Nibbles' grip was enough to allow Hootie to grab hold of the gun with his talons and fly off.

Nibbles was a student of the same fight philosophy school I was. He brought his knee up toward my groin, but I twisted my lower body, so he got the outside of my hip instead.

It still hurt.

"That shall be enough from both of you." The voice seemed to come from all around us and sounded like a cross between singing and robotic tones.

Nibble's face contorted more from that order than it had when I smashed it in with a two-by-four. He brought his hands down to his side, bowed his head, then stepped backward until he was out of my reach.

I turned to see the oddest-looking man I'd ever had the displeasure of being near. Dressed in a custom-tailored suit that probably cost as much as I made in a good six months, he had the aura of someone who was physically imposing. However, when you broke down his parts, it didn't add up. At maybe six-five, he was ridiculously thin, like a scarecrow someone forgot to put all the stuffing in. His fingers seemed too long, like they should have an extra knuckle. The shoes on his feet were expensive but so big they wouldn't have looked out of place on a clown. By far, the most disturbing part of him was his head. Big was an understatement. It seemed too long from chin to top. Its chiseled jaw was too narrow for a person and ended in a point. Even his eyes were odd, round and double the size they should have been, with the barest bump in the spot where a nose should sit.

It was as if a kindergartner had tried to build a man but really wanted milk and cookies, so just made up some of the proportions to get done quicker. Bighead took a step closer, and his legs seemed to move in unnatural ways, almost as if a frog decided to walk upright. Just the sight of him coming near freaked me out.

He had the same effect on Wayne and Hootie. Either of them could have flown away but instead held each other for comfort, which would have been cute at any other time, given their disparaging sizes.

I then realized that the guy who ran this operation hadn't been born with his name. He either chose it or had it thrust upon him by someone who spoke Spanish.

"Mr. Cabeza, I assume."

"For a hairless primate, you assume a lot, especially after interfering in my operation. It ends now."

I nodded enthusiastically. "Absolutely. The dingbat, batsquatch, and I will leave, and you'll never see us again."

"You're not permitted to steal my property."

"Intelligent beings aren't property. In case you've forgotten, slavery is illegal in this country."

"Such faith is misplaced. Your authorities would rule that they are animals, and animals can be owned."

"Agree to disagree."

"I do not have to agree to anything."

Nibbles cleared his throat. "Excuse me, Mr. Cabeza, but you want me to kill this fool and dispose of the body?"

"Disposing of the body is the least of our concerns. After all, our fighters need to be fed."

I didn't like the sound of that. Pigs have been fed murder victims to dispose of the remains, so I suppose there was no reason why cryptids couldn't be used for the same thing.

"And killing is far too lenient a punishment for someone who has inconvenienced me. We shall simply add him to the night's entertainment. I think he shall particularly despise the situation when he realizes the beast he came to save may be the one to slaughter him."

"You're the boss, sir, but may I point out something that appears like it may become an issue?" Nibbles said, looking far more nervous than he had in either of our fights.

Mr. Cabeza gave his underling a look that was part amusement and part disdain for daring to imply he had missed something. Cabeza waved his hand in a circle, motioning for Nibbles to get on with it. "Go on."

"By letting paying customers see what happens to him, it gives them power over us should they decide to threaten us with squealing to the cops."

Cabeza nodded his head as if to indicate that the question hadn't been a total waste of his time. "That is one way of looking at. Another is that by watching his death and doing nothing, they become co-conspirators. It will give some a rush and give us a hold over others when we point out that by not having reported anything immediately, they all are accessories to his murder."

"You both obviously have a lot to work out, and we don't want to hold you, so we'll be on our way." I stepped toward the door. Cabeza's only reaction was to pull out a cell phone and put a finger on the screen.

I don't know what happened, but Wayne and Hootie collapsed to the ground writhing in pain, trying to cover their ears.

"What are you doing to them?"

"Simply reminding them who is in charge here." Cabeza fiddled with his phone screen some more. "Something you are about to learn."

His long slender fingers turned the screen toward me. It got so bright that solid light seemed to shoot right toward my face.

Everything went white before my world faded to black.

CHAPTER SEVENTEEN

A buzzing shot through my head, trying to wake me up. I reached to hit the snooze button then wondered why there was so much sand in my bed. And why was it on fire? Although the flying was neat.

Somewhere along the way, I realized it was vitally important that I fully wake up.

I regretted it instantly. On the plus side, the sight instilled terror in my soul, which took me from drowsy to feeling like I'd drunk a double espresso in a heartbeat. A huge humanoid lizard was spitting flaming loogies at me. The sensation of flying had been Wayne tossing me through the air out of the path of a fireball.

I'd never seen anything like the creature before, but judging by the crowd's chanting, it was the cherufe from the fight poster. It had a good foot of height on the batsquatch, not to mention the whole spitting fireball thing. I reached for the pepper spray or homemade stun gun only to realize not only were both gone, but I didn't even have the jacket. I was in a short-sleeved dress shirt, minus the padding.

When the next lava loogie launched at me, I ran toward Mr. Lizard, dove in the space between his legs, rolled back to my feet, then kept running. I guess the fire-spitting lizard man wasn't expecting the direct approach, so I managed to get behind him and stomp on his tail while pulling my belt off. I climbed up his back and threw my belt around his neck and pulled.

I'd never wanted to be a cowboy, but suddenly I was in a rodeo nightmare, with a lizard trying to throw me off instead of a bronco.

I managed to stay on his back for a few seconds before thudding to the ground. I rolled as soon as I hit. The next lava loogie missed me by a couple of feet, but the heat of it incinerated some of my arm hairs.

I grabbed two handfuls of sand and hurled them at Mr. Lizard's eyes. It blinded him long enough for me to run to the far end of the battle cage, where I dodged a rod thrust from outside the fence.

Tall Drink enthusiastically tried to jab me with one of the long electric prods. I grabbed hold of the middle of the zapper and pulled, slamming him into the fence. Tall Drink pushed the button, grinning. The current surged behind me, but since I wasn't touching the metal prongs, I didn't get zapped.

I dropped to the floor while pinning the prod to my side and holding on for dear life. The weight of my fall pulled the shocker free of Tall Drink's grasp. Brooklyn smacked him in the back of the head, and I could see Mr. Cabeza sitting back in the shadows on his armchair throne, watching it all.

Bighead was grinning, so I flipped him off and got back to the matter at hand.

Hootie was zipping back and forth through the air like a pinball as a three-legged creature rose to the top of the cage, its legs somehow stretching. It looked like a living tripod, but one leg was actually a tail that dragged along the sand. It ran awkwardly and slammed itself down to the floor by shrinking its legs and tail in an attempt to squash the dingbat. Fortunately, Hootie was faster, and Tripod's body slam missed.

Wayne ran interference, doing his best to stay out of the other cryptids' way while keeping Hootie and me from getting hurt. He had no interest in fighting and was being booed by the crowd because of it.

"Look out!" I screamed, but it was too late.

Brooklyn reached into the cage with a giant version of a catchpole, the things with the collapsible collars that dog catchers used on strays. It wrapped around Wayne's throat. The goon yanked the unsuspecting batsquatch back into the fence. Dr. Cliff plunged a needle into Wayne's shoulder before pushing down the plunger on a syringe.

The evil vet answered my glare with a grin.

"A little cocktail of my own creation to make uncooperative beasts more aggressive. It ups the entertainment value. It's amazing what a little ephedrine, acepromazine, and dexamethasone will do to an otherwise calm and pleasant creature. In about ninety seconds, your friend is going to kill you."

"Bitch."

If Dr. Cliff was to be believed, the only cryptid in here that I wouldn't have to worry about fighting was Hootie.

Going with the assumption that Tripod was the tripodero that Hootie was supposed to fight, I wasn't giving my survival good odds. They got worse when I saw the tripodero's snout shoot booger darts toward Hootie, contracting like a pump-action shotgun before each snot shot. If what I overheard was accurate, those tiny darts were powerful enough to wound humans, and both of the cryptids on the other side ate human flesh.

So far, Tripod hadn't hit the dingbat, but that couldn't last forever. The tripodero seemed to be the cryptid I had the best shot of taking out, so I went after it, well aware that one of those snout shots had taken out another man's eye.

Tripod was so focused on Hootie it didn't notice as I tackled one of its tall, thin legs. I'd hoped to bring it down, but things didn't work out exactly as planned.

Sure, Tripod came down all right, but on top of me. Fortunately, it only knocked me to the side. Otherwise, I think the impact would have killed me. I didn't get up fast enough and got snout shot in my shoulder.

The smell of my blood seemed to excite Tripod. It swiveled toward me. As its snout contracted again, I zapped its nearest leg with the electric prod. It convulsed, so I jolted it again, then kicked it in the head a few times to make sure it was knocked out.

I turned toward the cherufe, figuring the lava-spitting giant lizard man as the next biggest threat. It's amazing how wrong I was.

A ferocious roar sounded behind me, and I was bowled over as Wayne shoved past to plow into the cherufe, who, as you can imagine, did not take the attack well. The pair clamped onto each other and began rolling around in the pit to the cheers of the crowd.

Hootie hovered next to me.

"Has he ever been like this before?"

The antlered bird shook his head.

One of the lava loogies landed beside us, super-heating the surrounding sand into glass.

I debated about using my foot to try to smash the glass, so I had something with an edge to use against Mr. Lizard or getting closer to help Wayne by zapping the cherufe, but they were wrestling and tumbling too fiercely, each trying to sink their teeth into the other. One misstep, and I'd be crushed. Or worse.

Wayne seemed to gain the upper claw and got on top of his opponent just as Mr. Lizard's launched another load of flaming lava snot. The batsquatch leapt up while flapping his bat wings so it missed him and landed a few feet from the cage fence, which gave me an idea.

It would cost me my sole weapon, but it was the only thing I'd come up with that had even a chance of getting any of us out of this fight cage.

I stuck the business end of the zapper into the sand beneath the still-glowing lava loogie. Coming up from beneath it, I hoped the molten glass might act as a shield for the zapper long enough for this to work.

Using the six-foot-long prod as a combination lever and catapult, I scooped the blistering loogie and hurled it about ten feet up onto the metal fence where it stuck, however briefly. Then it fell downward, melting away the fence links as it dropped.

The Tripod's legs shrunk when it was knocked out, but now they twitched. I had to get rid of it before it woke up. I rushed over to grab its back. Then, spinning like a hammer thrower, I hurled it out the opening.

Landing on what passed for its feet, it shot up to about twelve feet high, then ran over the table service area and began slamming down on furniture and people alike.

It wasn't pretty and caused the crowd to stampede.

"Hootie, I need you to distract Wayne so I can get Mr. Lizard over there to go outside the cage."

There was a high-pitched hoot before the dingbat zipped to buzz around the batsquatch's head. One blue hand then the other swatted again and again, but Wayne wasn't fast enough to lay a claw on Hootie.

I started waving my arms to get the attention of the cryptid with breath so bad it burned. "Hey, Mr. Lizard, come and get me."

The cherufe charged, and I held the electric prod up in front of me. It was covered in glass and partly melted but still recognizable. Mr. Lizard probably had it used on him enough times to be wary of it. In fact, he stopped.

Here's hoping Mr. Lizard was sentient too.

"You can stay here and fight me, or you can go out there to get even with the people who did this to you. Your call."

I swear Mr. Lizard gave a deep chuckle as his mouth turned up into a grin full of sharp teeth. He spat twice, each one of the loogies smaller than the ones he'd been spitting earlier but no cooler. They hit the fence on either side of the first opening. They melted the metal, forming an even bigger hole, which he marched through.

The cherufe jumped up on a table, tilted his head back, and roared. Those who hadn't been stampeding decided that now was an excellent time to join in.

Mr. Lizard spun while spitting around the room, hitting the ceiling, walls, and floor. These lava loogies were even smaller, maybe the size of baseballs, but still ridiculously hot. It wasn't going to take long for the whole building to catch fire.

I followed Mr. Lizard out of the fight cage, looking over my wounded shoulder to see that the dingbat still buzzed around the batsquatch, keeping his focus away from everybody else. The crowd's screaming grew louder as the Tripod marched above the stampede, sending its snout darts into random people. Or maybe not so random. Tall Drink and Brooklyn were among the first wounded, and each was hit with several shots. Both would need at least one eye patch.

Mr. Cabeza sat in his chair, shaking his head at the chaos. That was good. It meant he didn't see me sneaking up behind him.

When he started messing with his phone again, I rushed forward and swung the zapper down on his hand. His phone clattered to the ground, the glass shattering from the tip of the prod. I rammed the business end into his throat and pressed the trigger button. To my complete and utter amazement, the prod still worked. Cabeza twitched and collapsed into his chair. I grabbed his phone as I hit the trigger again, then one more time for good measure.

Plumes of smoke billowed through the warehouse. We needed to get out. I couldn't spot the evil vet, Cueball, or Nibbles anywhere in the panicked crowd. I hoped they were too busy to worry about little old me.

I ran back into the battle cage and was charged by the batsquatch for my trouble. Wayne tossed me to the ground like I was a rag doll and jumped down after me, straddling my body with his legs. An open claw rose up behind his head, ready to slice down.

For a moment, I toyed with the idea of using the phone in my hand to knock him out, but it was like no operating system I'd ever seen before. It was all symbols, no English. And to be honest, I had no idea which button would do the trick.

"Wayne, stop! Don't hurt me. Remember, I'm your friend." My shout made the big blue furry guy freeze and blink. "I know you don't want to hurt me. It's just the drugs that evil vet gave you. You want to be a hero, remember? Heroes don't kill their friends. You need to snap out of this. We need to get out. The building's on fire."

Wayne calmed but just didn't seem to care anymore. I've rarely seen such a look of despair. The poor guy looked like he had given up on everything. There was still something that might motivate him.

"If we get out, you'll be free."

Both arms came at me faster than I'd seen any blow move before. I figured I was hamburger.

I wasn't. Instead, I was enveloped by a pair of blue furry arms as Wayne barreled toward the hole in the fight cage. Despite the chemicals messing up his head, he managed to take flight over the crowd and get us out the door ahead of most of them. Hootie beat us outside.

Wayne pointed to me.

"I'm okay. We need to get out of here." Wayne shook his head. "Why not?"

Wayne stood up tall with his hands on his hips.

I looked around at the chaos. People were turning on each other to get out the one door because it had been rigged to restrict access. Any second, they'd be trampling each other.

"You need to get away. This is no time to be a hero."

The big blue guy smiled, nodded as if telling me that yes, it was. Then he winked at me.

Wayne grabbed hold of a stop sign post with both blue hands. He wiggled it back and forth until the metal at the bottom snapped. The batsquatch leapt to a section of wall about ten feet from the door and swung the metal bar like a sledgehammer.

In less than a minute, it made a hole. Using his hands, Wayne expanded it enough for people to come out three at a time. And come out, they did.

Wayne flew twenty feet further down the building and did the same thing. The batsquatch continued until there were enough holes in the wall for all the people to get out safely.

The Tripod came out one, shot up to twenty feet, and started lunging across the parking lot. It stopped halfway across it to smash down on a red Ferrari. It enjoyed that so much it kept doing it to other cars, including to one particular rented Verde Mantis Lamborghini.

I was so glad I took the insurance.

Mr. Cabeza casually strolled out one of the holes Wayne made, ineffectively trying to lose himself in the crowd. He was taller than most of the people, and his big head was too easy to recognize.

"It's Cabeza!" I shouted, pointing to the owner of Spot 51 as I ran after him. Wayne flew and landed in front of him, cutting him off, so Bighead ran away from the parking lot.

I was impressed. This guy could give Usain Bolt a run for his money. Cabeza made it all the way to the back of the warehouse, which was unlit, as the flames hadn't reached back that far yet. Unsurprisingly, Hootie reached him first and dive-bombed to rip off something from the top of Cabeza's head.

I guess Bighead wore a toupee.

The batsquatch landed, swinging the stop sign. Somehow Cabeza went full Matrix and bent over backward to avoid the blow.

"Stop this nonsense, or I will hurt the lot of you," Cabeza said, sounding totally confident as he stood in the shadows.

"I don't think so, but just for fun, how about I start pressing some buttons on this phone while pointing it at you?"

I couldn't make out his features, but Cabeza did bring up a long, slender hand to stroke his chin. "That would be more dangerous than a drunken chimpanzee playing with a nuclear weapon. Here's my counteroffer—give me back my phone and not only will I let you live, but I will transfer ownership of the batsquatch and dingbat to you and give you my word that no one in my organization will bother you so long as you leave us alone."

"Or how about this as a counter-counteroffer—we beat the crap out of you and turn you over to the cops."

"The police won't bother me. I'll be long gone before any law enforcement arrives," Cabeza said.

"Really? You call an Uber?"

"Something like that."

As if on cue, a light turned on in the sky above us. I looked up to see a flying saucer hovering over us. In the illumination, when I looked back down, I realized Hootie hadn't taken Cabeza's toupee—he'd snatched his entire face like it was a mask at the end of a Scooby-Doo episode.

Cabeza was an alien with gray skin, a big head, and enormous eyes that looked like two black pools.

"Would you like to reconsider my offer?"

I looked back up. The flying saucer was bigger than three city buses. I doubt my fists were going to do anything against it. "How do we know you'll keep your word?"

"You don't, but I do have the upper hand here. You might hit a button that would destroy me, but that ship will then take you on board to examine and torture. What other choice do you have?"

We took the deal.

CHAPTER EIGHTEEN

"You're telling me Mr. Cabeza got away in a flying saucer?" Tiffany was more flabbergasted than disbelieving.

"Yep. A beam of light sucked him up into the sky."

"What about Mr. Lizard and the Tripod?" Amber asked.

"The flying saucer flew over the lizard man, and the light sucked him up into the UFO too. I didn't see them get the tripodero, so maybe it got away." But I hoped not. The last thing my city needed was a flesh-eating monster on the loose. We had too many of the human monster variety already.

"But not before wrecking your rented Lamborghini?" Tiffany said.

I shrugged. "I wasn't exactly in a position to stop him."

"And you couldn't hand Cabeza something else and trick him into thinking it was his phone?" Amber said. "Because I think that phone sounds pretty dangerous, and I'm not sure someone like him should have it."

"I agree, but Cabeza was anything but stupid. And even if I kept it, I had no idea how to use it. Who knows what could happen if I hit the wrong button? I could kill somebody or blow something up."

"Maybe even the city," Tiffany whispered.

"Maybe even the planet," Amber said.

We all fell quiet for a moment.

"Still, he let us go, so I got something out of the trade."

Tiffany looked behind me at the main reasons she wasn't questioning any of my story. "And now you have to figure out how to take care of a batsquatch and a dingbat."

"A hero batsquatch and his sidekick," I said.

Both ladies had been very impressed when I told them about Wayne saving all the patrons who had gotten their jollies watching him and other cryptids battle.

The dingbat hooted in a loud tone, landed on the counter, pointed at his chest, shook his head, pointed at me, and nodded.

"What?" I said, confused.

Amber giggled. "Hootie's telling you he's not the sidekick. *You* are."

Before I could attempt a comeback, the door to the showroom opened, and Aunt Lizzie walked in. Technically, she is old enough to be our grandmother, but no one was going to call her a little old lady, even with her snow-white hair. She stood at six foot two inches and claimed to be proud of her age. Of course, no one we know has ever heard her admit what that age is. I will point out that at one point in her heyday, she hung out with the Rat Pack. It was, however, quite a bit after their heyday.

We all turned to look at Aunt Lizzie, who as always was elegantly dressed, today in a blue skirt and yellow blouse. She ignored the three humans. Her glance went up to the top of Wayne's furry head, then down to his blue feet before turning to take in Hootie. She wore a pair of glasses on a chain around her neck, which she put on to give them a twice over.

Calmly she took off and folded her glasses, then let them drop back onto her chest before turning to stare at my bloody shirt. "Rufus, is your shoulder all right?"

Amber had removed the pellet, then sutured and bandaged me up. "Yes, Aunt Lizzie."

"I'm glad to hear it. Now would you care to explain our two guests?"

"What makes you think it was me and not Amber or Tiffany?"

Aunt Lizzie crinkled her face then made a sound halfway between a cough and a chuckle.

"They followed me home. Can I keep them?" Then I explained what had happened, careful to leave out the part about letting the dingbat rest on her workbench.

Aunt Lizzie sighed, pressed her palm to her face, then plopped into her work chair. "And you've thought this through, have you?"

Amber and I nodded while Tiffany tried to fade into the background. Aunt Lizzie raised an eyebrow when the two cryptids also nodded.

"Where are they going to live?"

"Here in Exquizite," I said. Both Aunt Lizzie's eyebrows raised. She turned toward Amber.

"I'm okay with it."

"Did anyone think of consulting with *me* first to see if I was also okay with it?"

I could've pointed out to Aunt Lizzie that Amber owned the majority share of the business, and even without me agreeing, technically, she had the legal right to decide things like this. She and I both also knew that if we didn't get Aunt Lizzie on board, it would never end up working.

"Where exactly are they going to stay? Do we have another apartment area that I don't know about?"

"We can clear up a space in our storage area for them."

"What about their... biological needs? Will one of you be cleaning up after them? Are we going to be buying a tiger-size litter box?"

"They can both use the toilet," I said. Wayne had flown me back the full twenty miles, albeit with a rest break at a gas station where I showed him the finer points of indoor plumbing. Hootie was already aware of them.

"How are you planning on explaining their presence to our customers, not to mention the populace at large?"

"We think we've got that covered, thanks to Tiffany's brilliant idea," Amber said.

Aunt Lizzie's eyebrows shot up, and she turned her stare on Tiffany. My aunt is one of the few people I've ever seen intimidate Tiff.

"And this brilliant idea is what? Hide them and have them only come out at night?"

Tiffany pulled her shoulders back, stood up straighter, and pulled down on her blazer. "No. Hiding someone as large as Wayne in an urban area for an extended period isn't sustainable without restricting his freedom." It went unsaid that freedom was the entire reason Wayne and Hootie were here. "We have an advantage over most other urban areas. In Las Vegas, everything is larger-than-life. Instead of hiding, we put Wayne out into the casual public eye. We announce his existence, make him the mascot of Exquizite costumes." Hootie buzzed in front of her head, his hoots sounding like a yappy dog. "Along with Hootie, of course. We offer batsquatch costumes for rent and clip-on antlers for pets."

"Oh, joy. More pet costumes." It was one of our lines. "And who, pray tell, will be making these batsquatch costumes? As if I have to ask."

Amber pushed across a piece of paper she'd been sketching on. "I'll do most of the work, but if you're willing to help, we can make the outfits as realistic as possible, including high-end models with animatronic faces and wings."

"And why would I want to do that?"

Wayne stepped forward, his face contorted into something resembling a sad puppy dog. It was adorable. Hootie landed next to her and tried to do the same, but with the beak and feathers, his face just wasn't as expressive, although his eyes did seem to get bigger, particularly his pupils.

"Hmm. I remain unmoved by your sorrowful cuteness. How do I know the two of you are safe to have around?"

"They saved my—" Aunt Lizzie shut me up with a flick of her wrist and a flash of her palm toward my face.

"Rufus, I didn't ask you. I asked Wayne and Hootie."

Wayne crouched down and brought one of his wings in front of his face like it was a cape and, with an index finger, perked his ears to stand up straighter along each side of his head.

"You're Count Dracula? I'm afraid the idea of you trying to drink people's blood is not comforting."

Amber giggled. "No, Aunt Lizzie, he's trying to show you he's like Batman."

"Are you going to go around beating up people you think are bad guys?"

Wayne shook his head. Standing up straight, he placed his fists on his hips in a heroic pose.

"So, you're telling me you're a hero?"

"Well, he did save..."

Aunt Lizzie glared at me. "Rufus, I already told you I wanted them to tell me, not you. Why am I having to repeat myself?"

I bowed my head to make a quick examination of my shoes. "Sorry, Aunt Lizzie."

"Did you really save all those horrid people at the fight club?"

Wayne nodded.

"Good deeds should be rewarded but are you telling me you are a hero because of what you did?"

The batsquatch shook his head and wiggled one of his open hands from palm up to palm down.

"But you want to be a hero?"

Wayne tilted his head as Amber accidentally knocked her pencil on the floor. Wayne held an index finger and pointed to the pencil. He walked over, picked up the pencil, then handed it back to Amber.

"Ah." Aunt Lizzie smiled, a very good sign. "You want to help people."

The batsquatch nodded his head furiously. Hootie touched his chest with the tips of both wings.

Aunt Lizzie looked at the dingbat. "You too?"

Hootie's antlers bobbed up and down as he nodded.

"Very commendable. Both of you have better aspirations than most humans. You do understand that there may be some danger involved? This alien, Mr. Cabeza, may not keep his word and come back for you. The government or somebody who thinks you might make a fine addition to a show, be it highbrow or lowbrow, may try to kidnap you."

Both cryptids nodded.

"We could try to get both of you back to your homes instead."

Wayne teared up, and Hootie landed on his shoulder and wrapped his wings around his neck.

"You can't go home, can you?" I asked.

Wayne shook his head.

"You have a home with us as long as you want it," I said.

Aunt Lizzie cleared her throat and frowned in my direction.

"Come on, Aunt Lizzie. We all know you already made your decision before you offered to find their way home."

"You think you know me that well, Rufus?"

"Am I wrong?"

"You are not. So how are the two of you going to earn your keep? Food and rent aren't free, you know."

"They both already agreed to help me around the shop," Amber said. "With the speed that Hootie moves at, he can do a lot of things in a fraction of the time I could. Wayne can do the heavy lifting, not to mention stand outside and spin one of those signs to get the public used to seeing him without being shocked. It might drum up some business or at least some PR."

"Plus, they can both help me with cases. If we fit Hootie with a camera, he'd be able to do better surveillance than any drone. And if I ever needed extra muscle, I can't imagine anyone more intimidating than Wayne."

The batsquatch flexed like a bodybuilder at a show, which made his muscles look even bigger.

"I guess there is only one thing left to do. Wayne and Hootie, welcome to the family."

There were smiles on everyone's faces, human and otherwise.

"Let's go over a few ground rules." She looked at Hootie as if she knew. "First, nobody touches my workbench."

ABOUT THE AUTHOR

Patrick Thomas is the award-winning author of the beloved *Murphy's Lore* fantasy humor series, the darkly hilarious *Dear Cthulhu* advice empire and the creator of the *Agents of the Abyss* monster spy series.

His over 40 books include *Fairy Rides The Lightning, By Darkness Cursed, Lore & Dysorder, Dead to Rites, Startenders, As the Gears Turn,* and *Exile & Entrance.* He is the co-author of the long running *Mystic Investigators* paranormal mystery series. He co-wrote *The Santa Heist* and *Assassins' Ball* with John French.

His latest SF humor series kicks off with *Bikini Jones Vs. The Brain-nappers From Outer Space.* He co-edited *Camelot 13, New Blood, Hear Them Roar* and was an editor for *Fantastic Stories of the Imagination* and *Pirate Writings* magazines.

Over 100 of his stories have been published in magazines and anthologies. His noir novella appears in *Murder in Montague Falls. Dear Cthulhu* broadcasts monthly on the radio show *Destinies: The Voice of Science Fiction.* A number of his books were part of the props department of the CSI television show and *Nightcaps* was even thrown at a suspect's head. His *Fairy With A Gun* had been optioned for film and TV by Laurence Fishburne's Cinema Gypsy Productions. Top Men Productions made his *Soul For Hire* Story, *Act of Contrition,* into a short film.

He wrote the first two books in *The Wildsidhe Chronicles* YA series. As **PATRICK T. FIBBS,** he has penned the Ughabooz picture and first reader books as well as the middle reader books the *Babe B. Bear Mysteries, the Undead Kid Diaries,* and *Joy Reaper Checks Out* and the YA *Emotional Support Nightmare.*

Visit him online at www.patthomas.net and www.patricktfibbs.com.

artist's rendition of Batsquatch

BATSQUATCH

ORIGINS: First sighted after the eruption of Mount St. Helens, this cryptid seems centralized to the Pacific Northwest, with sightings primarily in the Cascade Mountains, Washington State, and California, but also reaching as far east as Ohio. However, there are noted accounts of flying primates going back as far as the sixteenth century all around the world. There is a marked similarity to these cryptids despite regional variation in names.

DESCRIPTION: While accounts vary, most agree this is a flying primate with blue fur and red or yellow eyes. The muzzle resembles that of a wolf, while the ears are batlike. It is also said to have bird-like feet. All accounts make mention of very sharp teeth.

Batsquatch (a melding of the words 'bat' and 'Sasquatch') stands between seven and nine feet tall and its leather-like wings have a fifty-foot wing span, with which it is able to fly very, very fast.

Another unusual trait ascribed to the Batsquatch is the ability to psychically interfere with technological items such as car engines and transmission devices such as televisions and radios.

LIFE CYCLE: Unknown.

HISTORY: The earliest recorded account of a Batsquatch sighting occurred in March 1980, in the aftermath of the eruption of Mount St. Helens.

Perhaps the creature awoke from a form of hibernation or the natural disaster dislodged the Batsquatch from a previously self-contained habitat.

These theories, of course, have yet to be substantiated.

Throughout the '90s all the way until recent days, there have been encounters with this powerful creature. These sightings have happened with sufficient regularity that some people in the region caution about going out after dark.

In 1994, a young man was driving in Pierce County, Washington when something caused his engine to stall. When he got out to check, something large landed on the hood, buckling it. When

artist's rendition of Dingbat

he looked, he found himself face to face with a snarling Batsquatch. He fled, reaching town with the back of his shirt shredded. When the vehicle was retrieved, the hood was dented and scratched, as if by clawed feet.

As recently as June 2021, a dawn encounter took place as a young woman hiking with her dog came face to face with this living legend on a trail in Ape Canyon (the site of a famous 1924 encounter where miners were besieged in their cabin one night by multiple Sasquatches.)

Both the woman and her dog survived the encounter, but this and other events have experts wondering decreased human activity is drawing out these and other cryptids, or are secret excrements encroached on their territory and driven them back into the public eye?

POSSIBLE VARIATIONS: The Ahool (Java), Ropen (New Guinea), Camazotz (Mesoamerica), and Orang Bati (Southeast Asia).

DINGBAT

ORIGINS: Theorized as one of the many hoax cryptids (such as the Wunk and the Squidgicum-Squee) perpetuated by the lumberjack community to heckle newcomers and frighten off unwanted hunting activity from the forests where the they made their livelihood. The Dingbat is found in the region of the Great Lakes.

DESCRIPTION: A hybrid of both mammal and bird, the Dingbat has a compact, feathered body, large wings, and short pronged antlers. In flight, it moves super fast.

This cryptid is known to torment hunters, snatch bullets out of the air, siphon gas from their vehicles, and pull pranks to annoy them.

LIFE CYCLE: Unknown.

HISTORY: Earliest mentions of the Dingbat appear in the late 19th to early 20th century.

ABOUT THE ARTIST

Although Jason Whitley has worn many creative hats, he is at heart a traditional illustrator and painter. With author James Chambers, Jason collaborates and illustrates the sometimes-prose, sometimes graphic novel, *The Midnight Hour,* which is being collected into one volume by eSpec Books. His and Scott Eckelaert's newspaper comic strip, Sea Urchins, has been collected into four volumes. Along with eSpec Books' Systema Paradoxa series, Jason is working on a crime noir graphic novel. His portrait of Charlotte Hawkins Brown is on display in the Charlotte Hawkins Brown Museum.

CAPTURE THE CRYPTIDS!

Cryptid Crate is a monthly subscription box filled with various cryptozoology and paranormal themed items to wear, display and collect. Expect a carefully curated box filled with creeptastic pieces from indie makers and artisans pertaining to bigfoot, sasquatch, UFOs, ghosts, and other cryptid and mysterious creatures (apparel, decor, media, etc).

http://CryptidCrate.com